HOOK
A No Prisoners MC Book Novella

by Lilly Atlas

Lilly Atlas Books

ISBN-10: 1-946068-12-8
ISBN-13: 978-1-946068-12-5

For all the readers who took a chance on making a writer's dream come true. Thank you!

After ten years away, Marcie finally ventures back to where she grew up. She isn't in town for twenty-four hours when she crosses paths with Hook and Striker, the two boys who kept her safe and happy as a young girl. Only they aren't boys anymore. They are fully grown, muscular, alpha men. Members of the No Prisoners Motorcycle Club. All through her teenage years, Marcie's heart belonged to Hook. Not that he ever seemed to notice. And it appears that as an adult, not much has changed with regard to her feelings toward the sexy biker. But a bossy, alpha man is not what independent Marcie is looking for.

The moment Hook lays eyes on Marcie, it's as though the last ten years apart never existed. Back when she was off limits, he wanted her, and it doesn't take long before he realizes he still wants her. Marcie's changed, though. She's no longer a frightened teenager in need of a haven. Now she's a beautiful, confident woman, and a bit too independent. Will Hook be able to convince Marcie a life with him wouldn't stifle her freedom? Their relationship is tested when Marcie clings to her hard-won life and when an aspect of that life threatens not only their future together, but their safety as well.

Table of Contents

HOOK
A No Prisoners MC
Novella

CHAPTER ONE

Marcie lifted the long-necked bottle to her lips and drank a sip of the warm, stale beer she'd been nursing for the past forty-five minutes. As the tepid liquid filled her mouth, she cringed and forced herself to swallow. The desire to finish the beverage had long fled, but she needed something to keep her hands and mind occupied. With a small grunt of disgust, she set it down on the table and let her gaze wander around the smoke-filled bar.

She'd rather be just about anywhere than in this bar, back in her hometown of Crystal Rock, Arizona, sitting next to the boyfriend she desired about as much as the lukewarm beer. It wasn't his fault. Timing sucked. They'd only been dating for two weeks when her mother passed. Really, she hadn't been all that interested in him, but it was nice to have something to do a few nights a week. Ugh, that sure sounded shallow. Poor Tanner had tried to coax her onto his lap, but that would have made her look dependent on him for comfort. And she wasn't. She barely knew the guy.

For the first time in ten years, Marcie had made the trip back to Arizona. She'd returned to bury her mother, a miserable woman who spent the majority of Marcie's childhood stoned and in bed with one random man or another. They hadn't spoken in almost five years, and while she wasn't surprised to learn of her mother's passing, Marcie was truly shocked to discover what little the woman possessed was left to her only child.

A second shock came when her new boyfriend—if she could even give him the strong label—Tanner, offered to accompany her from Seattle to the unassuming town of Crystal Rock, claiming he wanted to assist in settling her mother's affairs. The show of support touched her, and in a weak moment she caved to his request. Had she been in her right mind, she'd have turned him down. His help wasn't necessary. She could handle the trip and her mother's meager affairs on her own, as she handled everything else life threw at her. Independently. Alone. Lonely.

But Tanner insisted, and for the first time in years, she'd relented and allowed someone the possibility to take care of her. And she'd been secretly relieved by the knowledge that she wouldn't have to make the journey alone. That was until he invited two of his friends, and turned the trip into a bro's trip complete with a two-night stop in Vegas.

From the moment Tanner hit the gas and left Seattle in the dust, aspects of his personality she hadn't yet been introduced to began to emerge. Unfortunately, he transformed into an overgrown frat boy would couldn't see past his next drink. Even his buddies Cameron and Billy seemed surprised by his slide back to his college days. What did she expect? This is what she got for giving a man she just met some control over her life.

His party mentality wasn't impressive and she wasn't the type to overlook poor behavior on the off chance it would improve with time. Nope, she was done with him.

The kind thing would be to just inform him tonight that they were through, but her brain was fried and she'd much rather do it back in Seattle, and not in a town where more bad than good memories lurked around every corner.

So, she'd end it as soon as they returned, and she'd be on her own once again. And wasn't that just how she liked it? It wasn't the eighteen hundreds. She could and would take care of herself. Too much of her childhood was spent afraid and cowering behind the protection and care of two very special friends. Now, she lived how she wanted without depending on anyone for anything.

Fatigue weighed heavy on Marcie's shoulders. She'd spent eight hours, today, sifting through a run-down trailer full of tragic childhood memories, and that was after a very simple and unattended burial service. Spending another night with three men who were happiest in whichever bar was closest was about as appealing as a trip to the gynecologist.

Glancing down at her lap, she smoothed the front of the simple, yet elegant, black skirt she'd worn with a black blouse to the lonely burial. Marcie had been the only person in attendance, unable to wake a hung-over Tanner before she had to leave. Her prostitute mother hadn't had true friends, and had alienated her family, so Marcie was it.

Tanner downed his own drink then grabbed her abandoned beer to polish that off as well. He clanked her beer bottle on the table and she jolted, lost in her own melancholy thoughts. "Damnit, Marcie, this is piss warm. Go grab me a new one from the bar." As he spoke he gave an unaffectionate tug on her short blonde hair. "I gotta take a piss. Where the hell's the john?" He glanced around the crowded bar. "Jesus, there's so many people here it's gonna take me a year to get to the damn can."

Marcie shot him a death look, but refused to allow him the satisfaction of seeing her rub the sore spot on her head. Tanner had been in a rotten mood all day, complaining about being stuck in Crystal Rock with nothing to do while Marcie dealt with her mother's personal effects. God forbid he offered to help. Not that she need it. She handled it without him. If she had enough energy to deal with the fallout, she'd just walk away tonight, but she couldn't handle a confrontation right now.

Relief was almost immediate as she left the three men at the table. The one and only reason she followed his command to grab a beer was to get away from them a few minutes. Tanner was right about one thing. The place was jam packed. It took quite a bit of fancy maneuvering to work her way to the bar without rubbing up on every body in the place.

With a heavy sigh, she took a seat at the bar, in no rush to grab the attention of the cute bartender.

A commotion from the opposite side of the dimly-lit bar caught her attention, and she turned in time to see a group of large, gruff bikers enter the establishment. Growing up in Crystal Rock, there was no way to escape knowledge of the No Prisoners motorcycle club. They ran the town, and had always patronized Black's as their bar of choice.

No surprise, the tattooed men in leather were accompanied by a gaggle of women with tiny skirts and even smaller tops, leaving less than nothing to the imagination.

"What'll it be, darlin'?" the young, thin man slinging bar asked with a flirty smile, most likely hoping to garner a larger tip. A bull ring ran through his septum and his hands, resting on the surface of the bar, had the words *game over* tattooed across the knuckles.

"Another please," she said, indicating the bottle she'd returned.

"Sure thing, sweetness. Be right back." He winked as he turned to grab her beer. Shaggy dark hair stuck out from under a backward baseball cap and his tan was nicely on display around his dark gray wife beater. Obviously, this was a casual establishment.

She smiled, charmed by his friendly nature. Crystal Rock boasted an eclectic mix of people from all walks of life. A few seconds later, he returned with the uncapped beer and another flirty wink. Marcie paid and swiveled on the stool. She'd stalled long enough. Time to rejoin the bromance at her table.

"Holy shit! Marcie? Marcie Barringer?" The voice was familiar, but she couldn't quite place it.

She whirled around, and came face-to-face, well, face-to-chest —the man was tall as a building—with Dylan Parker.

"Dylan?" she asked, unable to keep the delight from her voice. Without thinking, she launched herself off the stool, landed against his hard chest with a grunt, and wrapped her arms tightly around the body that was no longer that of a young boy, but a full-grown man. And a hot one at that.

He seemed just as elated to have run into her, and returned the embrace with gusto. "I can't believe it, Marce," he said, gripping her arms and holding her away from his body. He raked her up and down with his eyes. "Damn girl, you grew up into something gorgeous. I like that pixie cut. Fits you."

Marcie blushed, but couldn't remove the giant grin from her face. She'd known Dylan for as long as she could remember. Without him, she may not have survived her childhood, at least not in one piece. Neither of them had any siblings, and, being six years older, Dylan had appointed himself her surrogate older brother and protector.

He was the one person from her childhood that she could remember truly caring about her. It was a sibling kind of love, and she hadn't seen him since the day she left Crystal Rock almost ten years prior. The boy grew up in to one hell of a sexy man, and apparently was now a member of the motorcycle club, if the leather cut he wore was any indication.

She could barely believe he was here, in front of her. Time melted away at being near her surrogate big brother and she felt as if the past ten years had never occurred. He was tall, muscular, and deadly looking, with dark, almost black hair and chiseled features that made him look every bit the dangerous man he probably was now. The thought made her laugh. She knew way too much about him to ever consider him a danger, at least not to her.

Damn, it was good to see him.

"I can't believe I ran into you, Dylan," she said, giving him another quick squeeze.

"It's Striker now, babe." An arrogant smirk played across his lips.

"Striker?"

"Handle given to me by the club, on account of my impressive skills." A teasing glint lit his eyes and he bounced on the balls of his feet, fists up in a boxer's stance. He was forever getting into fights as a kid. As he'd grown into his teens, he'd put that energy to good use learning to box, and becoming quite proficient in the sport.

"Striker it is, then," Marcie returned.

"What are you doing here, hon? How long are you in town?" he asked, genuine concern filling his voice.

That concern was so familiar, a warmth she hadn't experienced in far too long bloomed in Marcie's chest. As long as he'd known her, he'd been concerned about her wellbeing, and at the time she'd been too young to appreciate the rarity of a man who wanted nothing more from her than her happiness. Marcie shrugged. "My mom passed. I'm here for a few days dealing with the details."

Striker grimaced. He'd had a front row seat to the shit show that was Marcie's childhood, and knew full well what a deadbeat her mother had been. "Shit, Marce. I wish I'd known. I'd have offered to help you. Is there anything I can do now?"

"No, Striker, there isn't much left and I can handle it."

He slung an arm around her shoulders and steered her back to the bar. "Well then, we at least need to have a drink or ten, while you're here. Wait until Hook sees you here. He's gonna flip his shit."

She raked her memory but came up with nothing. "Hook?"

Striker laughed. "My bad, honey. Man, I forget how long you've been away. Remind me to yell at you about that later." He gave her a playful scowl. "TJ."

Every last drop of saliva dried up until her mouth could rival the arid desert. TJ and Dylan, *Striker*, had been inseparable as teenagers and if she'd loved Striker as a brother, her tender young heart and innocent body had loved TJ in a very different way.

Hook

"Oh, there he is." Striker gestured toward the end of the bar. "Hey, Hook," he hollered over the music and loud chatter, getting the other man's attention. "Get your ass over here. Bet you a lap dance you won't believe who's here!"

Marcie was not in any way prepared for the punch to the gut she experienced when she got her first look at Hook in ten years.

Holy hotness. The man was the sexiest thing she'd ever laid eyes on. The boy had been every teenage girl's fantasy, but the man, the man was more than she'd dared to fantasize about.

Every feeling she'd ever had for the bad boy she lusted after as a teen came rushing back full force when that sinful mouth lifted in a wide, genuine smile.

CHAPTER TWO

Striker bellowed his name across the crowded-as-crap bar and Hook spun around. When he spotted Striker, he held up a hand in acknowledgement. Striker waved as he yelled for Hook to join him and some mystery guest.

What the hell? Striker wasn't one to get overly excited about much of anything. Snagging his frosty beer from the bar top, Hook strolled toward his friend. As he drew closer, he couldn't help but notice the nicely rounded backside of the woman Striker appeared very happy to talk to.

Damn, whoever she was, she sure looked good from the back. TJ felt a stirring in his groin and hitched his gait a bit, trying to adjust without being overtly obvious about it. Shit, he hoped Striker didn't want this broad, because that curvy ass was seriously turning him on and he just might be willing to give his brother a run for his money.

When he was within spitting distance, Striker called out, "You are never gonna guess who I ran into, brother." Placing his hands on the woman's arms, he turned her so TJ had a full-on view of the front of the woman this time.

Since he was a man, and currently sporting a semi, his gaze landed on her enticing full breasts before taking a slow journey up to her face. He noticed the amused glitter in her eyes before his brain registered whom the emerald green irises he was now staring into belonged to.

"Hello, *Hook*." Her soft voice danced along his aroused nerve endings, fueling his desire.

There was only one woman Hook had met with eyes that deep green color. "Marcie? No fuckin' way!"

Marcie threw back her head and let out a delighted laugh. The cheerful sound caused a further tightening in his pants. He needed to get himself under control. This was Marcie, for Christ's sake. She practically grew up in Striker's trailer. He didn't have enough fingers to count the number of nights as a teen he'd gone to hang at Striker's, only to find Marcie asleep on a mattress his buddy kept in his room just for her.

Her family life was shit growing up. Her junkie-whore of a mother didn't have a prayer of knowing who Marcie's father was. She'd traded sex for money and drugs and got knocked up by some asshole john who probably split town five seconds after he came.

Striker had carried a traumatized Marcie home with him one night after he'd discovered her struggling against one of her mother's *friends*. They lived in adjacent trailers and Striker had grown concerned by noises coming from Marcie's home. Luckily, he burst in before anything could happen, but Marcie had been shaken to the core. And she was ten.

After that, Marcie snuck out of her trailer to sleep at Striker's nearly every night. She never knew, but Striker called Hook after he'd gotten her settled. The two fifteen-year-old boys beat the shit out of the man that night, and a few others who'd looked a little too closely at her over the years.

She became a surrogate sister to Striker, and Hook helped look out for her through her teenage years as well. Unfortunately, he never felt very brotherly toward her, and the problem only intensified the older she got. A five-year age difference didn't mean squat now, but when he was twenty and she was fifteen, it sure did.

Now, it appeared nothing had changed, or maybe everything had changed. Marcie was all grown up, not a trace of the too-young girl left in her. "Christ, woman, you are smokin'."

A charming flush stole over Marcie's cheeks as Striker burst out laughing. "I told her the same thing."

Hook shot Striker a look over Marcie's shoulder that was none too friendly. The other man held up his hands in a pose of surrender as if to say, "she's all yours." But she sure as hell wasn't his. Shit, he hadn't even seen her in at least a decade, and here he was acting like a caveman in front of his best friend.

"You didn't exactly get hit with the ugly stick yourself, Hook." Marcie smiled and he swore he spied an answering desire in her gaze.

"Hey!" Striker's hands flew to his hips. "What the hell, woman?"

Marcie laughed, the sound stroking Hook's dick like a soft palm. "Sorry, Striker. You're very sexy, too." She patted Striker's cheek, her tone like she was placating a jealous child. Damn, it was good to see her.

Striker nodded with a pacified smile and Hook had the urge to smack the grin off his smug face. Striker appeared to relish Hook's discomfort. Bastard.

"So, what are you doing here, Marce?" Hook asked, falling back to the old nickname they'd called her as kids.

"Her mom died," Striker answered for her.

"Oh, I'm sorry, babe. I know you two weren't exactly close, but it still sucks."

"Thanks, Hook."

"Anything I can do?" He couldn't tear his attention from her gorgeous face. The same mesmerizing eyes and enticing lips he'd lusted after when he was young only grew more alluring with age. He needed to snap out of it before people started to notice him acting like a bitch in heat.

"There is," she said with a smile. "You can join me and Striker for a drink, or ten, as he put it."

Hook

"That, I can certainly do." A drink, and if he was a lucky son of a bitch, maybe something more, because Marcie wasn't a kid anymore and he'd wanted her for far too long.

CHAPTER THREE

Marcie kept her focus on Hook as he pivoted, snagged the attention of the bartender, and ordered another beer for himself. Her eyes fell to his ass, encased in snug low rider jeans, and she was afraid she might actually start drooling.

Shifting her stance, she felt the telltale dampness in her panties. Apparently, Hook still did it for her. Never had she had such an instantaneous physical reaction to a man. Trying to be discreet, she glanced down and noticed her now-hardened nipples were faintly visible through the fitted black blouse. Maybe he wouldn't notice. The lights were dim and the crowded space made it difficult to get a good, assessing look.

When she lifted her eyes, her gaze locked with Hook's, who, full beer in hand, had turned back to face her. Marcie froze, unable to tear her focus away from the heat in his eyes that told her he knew exactly what she'd been staring at.

Her back was to Striker, and luckily, he seemed oblivious to the sexual lightning strikes that now crackled between her and Hook.

Striker broke the spell, choosing that moment to sling an arm over her shoulders and tuck her against his side as he lifted his beer. "To long overdue reunions," he said.

"And to growing up," Hook added with a wink for Marcie.

She smiled and clinked the neck of her bottle against each of theirs. "*And* to sexy bikers."

Both men laughed which made her smile, and they chatted for a few minutes, filling her in on the motorcycle club, and regaling her with horror stories of their time as prospects for the club.

A lightness Marcie hadn't experienced in a very long time floated through her. Being with these two as they bantered back and forth, teasing her and ribbing each other, went a long way toward chasing away the loneliness that had plagued her for the past few years.

"So, Marce, fill us in on you. What are you up to these days? What are you doing for work? I love the hair." Hook fingered a short lock of her hair. Her mind immediately imagined him sliding his hands through it and guiding her head as she sucked him deep. Oookay, not time for those thoughts. She swallowed and tried to focus on his questions.

"Oh, I...uh, I sell drugs." She smiled to herself and waited for the reaction that never failed to disappoint.

Striker choked, and slammed his beer down on the bar while Marcie whacked him on the back.

A dark and thunderous expression rolled across Hook's face. "What the fuck, Marcie?" He practically yelled, but the sound was swallowed up by the rowdy bar patrons.

With a laugh, she made sure Striker could breathe before addressing Hook. "I'm a sales rep for a major pharmaceutical company. I visit doctors' offices and medical clinics, educating them on our products." She couldn't keep the shit-eating grin off her face. This felt so good, so familiar.

"Christ, woman." Hook shook his head. "Point to you for that one."

Striker mock glowered at her. "I forgot you could give as good as you get."

"By the way." She turned to Hook. "How much do I owe you for the beer?"

The glower he gave her had her barking out a laugh. "Please, woman. No way are you paying for the beer."

She frowned. Not acceptable. She wasn't a weak girl who needed to be taken care of anymore. And she wasn't a charity case. "I pay my own way. Always."

Hook cuffed her gently under the chin. "Not when you're out with us, you sure as fuck don't."

She rolled her eyes. This was why she hadn't called them when she arrived in town. Their need to protect, to take care of her, to take over her life. For six years, from the time she was ten until her mother moved them away at sixteen, she'd taken no responsibility for her life, allowing them to do just about damn near everything for her. Not anymore. "Really, Hook, I insist." She dug a five-dollar bill out of her back pocket and held it toward him.

"Noted." He winked at her as Striker snorted under his breath.

Since he obviously wasn't going to take the money, she shoved it down the front of his shirt. She rested her back against the bar and raised a challenging eyebrow.

Hook burst out laughing. "Okay, Miss Independent, you win that round. But don't think I won't find a way to get this back to you." He winked and moved closer to her, stretching his arm across the oak behind her. His hand lightly cupped the bare skin of her upper arm. The skin of his palm was warm and strong, callused and arousing, not like Tanner, whose hands were the soft hands of a tax attorney who detested physical labor.

Tanner.

Shit! He had to be back from the restroom by now.

She straightened and searched the thickening crowd, but couldn't see past the bodies to get eyes on their table. Seconds later, her gaze landed on the face of a very irritated Tanner as he wormed his way through the throng, straight toward the reunited trio.

How the hell could she have forgotten about Tanner? Jesus, she'd come over to the bar to grab him a beer. Instead of returning to him with it, she stayed at the bar, lusting over Hook, and drinking Tanner's entire beer. She just had this feeling the guy wasn't above making a scene in public, especially given all the alcohol he'd been putting away. If only the moron had shown his true colors a few days ago, she'd have dumped his ass. It would be over and done with.

The last thing Marcie wanted was for Tanner to get aggressive with Striker or Hook. Not only would she be mortified by the public display of manly tantrum, but she had no doubt that either of her old friends could annihilate him with minimal effort.

Please don't let it come to that.

Tense once again, the relaxed feeling of reminiscing with old friends obliterated by the scowl on Tanner's face, Marcie tried to shrug out of Hook's embrace. She took a step forward, but his sizable hand tightened around her arm. His hold didn't hurt, not in the least, but it was firm. The message was clear. He had no intention of letting her go. Ugh, this train was on the fast track to shit town.

Hook became aware the moment Marcie tensed next to him. She had been relaxed, lightly leaning into his body, and joking with him and Striker like no time had passed. Catching up with her was the most fun he'd had in quite a while. The feel of her lithe body pressed against him, even in such a platonic way had him thinking all sorts of dirty thoughts.

Then, like the flip of a switch, she grew rigid under his arm. He peered down to find a look of dismay on her pretty face. What was that about? Glancing up, he couldn't miss the angry male shouldering his way through the happy drinkers, a look of fury on his pretty-boy mug.

Marcie attempted to maneuver away from him, but Hook wasn't having that. There was no way he was letting whoever this asshole was upset her.

The man caught Striker's attention as well. Striker stepped in front of Marcie, blocking the bastard's path before he was within grabbing distance of her.

Ten minutes in her presence and the two of them were falling back into old habits of standing between Marcie and the evils of the world. It felt good. It felt right.

"Get the fuck out of my way, dude." The man snarled at Striker.

"Not gonna happen, *dude*." Striker stood in a loose pose, meant to deceive the world into thinking he wasn't a lethal fighter.

"You do not want to get in between me and my woman." The idiot was up in Striker's face now.

About four inches shorter than Striker, he was lean and athletic looking, but his physique was the type honed on the racquet ball court or golf course as opposed to Striker and Hook whose muscles came from working on bikes and MMA training.

Hearing the guy call Marcie his woman surprised Hook, and he looked down at her with a quirked brow. She looked like she wanted to sink into the ground, face red with embarrassment and eyes pleading.

"Please, Hook, it's okay. He's here with me," she whispered.

It didn't escape Hook's notice that Marcie didn't call him her boyfriend or any other possessive label, just said they were in the bar together. "Bro, Marce says he's cool."

Striker turned gauging for himself whether that was true, but he moved slightly, letting the man see Marcie.

Partly because he enjoyed the feel of her, and partly because provoking this guy gave him a thrill, Hook didn't release her. Instead, he stroked the ball of her shoulder like he had every right to his hand on her.

"Hey, Tanner. I came to get your beer, and ran into some friends I haven't seen since I moved away." Marcie's voice was light and breezy. "This is Striker." She pointed at Striker. "And this is Hook. Striker lived next door to me growing up and Hook is his best friend."

Hook didn't care for the phony cheerful quality in her voice. So what if she didn't get this overgrown baby's beer to him when he snapped his fingers? The dude should be getting his own damn beer, and Marcie's.

He and Striker both nodded at Tanner, but neither moved to shake his hand. Tanner didn't seem eager to get friendly either, blatantly ignoring them and focusing on Marcie.

"Let's go, Marcie. Billy's taking a piss then we're gonna bug out. I'm tired of this shit bar. Hell, I'm tired of this shit town."

"Sure, okay." Marcie looked at Hook and raised an eyebrow. He supposed that was code for *time to let me go*.

After he released her, she hugged Striker. "So good to see you, Dylan." She stressed his name and Striker smiled.

"You too, TJ," she said in a low tone as she slid her arms around his waist. Christ, he hadn't been called TJ in almost as long as she'd been gone. The name sounded nice on her lips.

He wrapped his arms around her in an embrace that was too familiar for just an old friend. Her soft breasts pillowed against his upper stomach, the pebbled nipples searing him like two lasers. His cock twitched in his pants. There was no way Marcie could have missed it; it was like a live animal clawing to be free. She stiffened slightly but didn't give any other indication as to the intimacy of the hug.

Hook kept his focus over her head, glaring at Tanner, whose jaw was clenched. He slid his hands down her back, resting them just inches above her ass. Tanner's jaw ticked, but the pussy didn't seem to have the balls to do anything more.

Striker cleared his throat and Hook backed off. The game was fun, but not if it would cause trouble for Marcie after she left.

Releasing her, he bent down and whispered in her ear. "You okay with this guy, gorgeous?"

"Yes of course. I can't tell you how good it was to see you. Sorry we didn't have longer to catch up." She gifted him a smile, but it didn't reach her eyes. She was not the same woman he'd been talking to five minutes ago. She was a tense, uncomfortable version of the typically vivacious Marcie, and Hook didn't care for it at all.

She didn't leave him much of a choice, so Hook stepped back and watched her walk away. Tanner moved in next to her and wrapped his arm around her upper arm in the same spot Hook had his hand just seconds before.

Hook met Striker's stare and wasn't surprised to see anger reflected at him. "What the fuck was that, brother? Looks a little bit like you were trying to mark some territory that ain't yours. Only thing you were missing was the leg lift."

Hook shrugged. "Didn't like the asshole. Come on, you can't tell me you didn't notice the change in her when he came over."

"No, I noticed it." Striker frowned. "Think we should follow them?"

"Nah, she's a big girl. She can go out with whoever she wants." Hook turned toward the bar. He needed a fuckin' drink.

Striker snorted. "So says the man who looked at her like he was a junkyard dog and she was a juicy steak."

More like he was a horny man and she was the woman whose brains he wanted fuck out. No need for the analogy. When he didn't reply, Striker laughed.

"Jack," Hook said to the bartender. "Double."

CHAPTER FOUR

Marcie stood in the dingy bathroom of the only motel within tens of miles of Crystal Rock. Her hometown itself didn't boast any lodging, so they were forced stay outside of town, in the Tortoise Inn, an old ramshackle motel with six drab rooms and zero amenities. Unless you counted the ability to rent a room by the hour an amenity.

With the scratchy, cardboard-quality motel towel tucked around her body, she gazed at her reflection in the mirror. She rubbed the cracked mirror in a circular motion, clearing the steam. The woman staring back at her had tired eyes and a sadness that spoke to how lost she was feeling. Though they weren't close, her mother's passing only exacerbated the feeling. The woman in the mirror hadn't felt right in a long while and seeing Striker and Hook last night clued her in to why.

She was lonely. Bone-deep lonely.

Sure, she had friends, but she was lonesome for family. For people who knew her. Really knew her—good, bad, and ugly. None of those people were in Seattle. Even after ten years of living there, she hadn't made strong, lifelong connections. Her own fault. So focused on fostering her independence, making a life for herself, and being self-sufficient, she managed to alienate virtually everyone she met.

Striker and Hook already knew her flaws, secrets, fears. They had lived the unpleasantness with her, and cared for her anyway.

But they'd coddled her for years, and she didn't need that anymore. Didn't need anyone to run her life. Somehow, she had to find a balance of relationships, both platonic and romantic, and independence so she could begin to develop a social life and find some contentment.

She cringed at the reflection, her eyes locking in on the three new finger-shaped bruises ringing her right upper arm.

It was no mystery to Marcie why Tanner had grabbed her in the same spot as Hook. He may have held her in the same location, but that's where the similarities ended. Whereas Hook's large, calloused hand felt warm and arousing, Tanner dug his fingers into the delicate skin of her arm with a force that had nearly made her stumble. She'd barely been able to tolerate the pain long enough to leave the bar without a scene. No doubt, had Hook or Striker noticed, a brawl would have broken out, and that was the last thing she wanted to deal with after such an emotionally draining day.

Not to mention she didn't need them to fight her battles. She'd shoved out of Tanner's hold and gave him hell in the parking lot, at least until his friends emerged from the bar. He was quiet and contrite on the taxi ride to the motel. She'd been prepared to pick up where she left off and tear him a new one when they arrived at their room, but he'd been dead asleep after she made a quick trip to the bathroom.

Her boss had introduced her to Tanner at a company barbecue; the two men had been roommates in college and remained close friends. She chatted with him for a while at the party, found him mildly interesting and his GQ looks appealing. He was flirty and sweet and by the end of the party had asked her to dinner. At the time, she'd thought he could be a good place to start. Go on some dates, make some new connections. See where it led.

Marcie really didn't date very much. The only example of man-woman relationships she'd been privy to growing up were beyond dysfunctional. Cash for sex and abusive drunks. Not exactly Disney movie love. Striker's home life was pretty on par with hers, but he'd been older and better equipped to handle it, and she'd never spent much time around Hook's family.

More than one john had beaten her mother, stolen from her, come on to Marcie, and generally treated her like shit. As a result, Marcie had a hard time trusting people, particularly men and tended to avoid close relationships with them. It was no mystery as to why she'd become so fiercely, and admittedly over the top, independent.

She'd only slept with two men in her twenty-six years, Tanner being the second. For a few weeks, she'd hoped Tanner could cure some of the solitude that seeped its way into her life, but that was turning out to be not the case at all.

He wouldn't care beyond the ego-bruise associated with being dumped. Heartbreak wouldn't be an issue since there wasn't really any substantial emotional connection between them. After only a few weeks, the L-word hadn't even crossed her mind, and she'd bet money on the fact that he wasn't nervously awaiting the right time to profess his own love.

Tanner pounded on the paper-thin door, and Marcie jumped so hard she nearly dropped the abrasive towel. "Unlock the fucking door, Marcie."

What the hell? His tone was one she'd never heard from him, nasty, almost violent. She twisted the flimsy lock and barely had time to draw her hand back before the door flew open, smacking against the wall with a crack. Bits of plaster flew into the small space. Tanner burst in, allowing Marcie no time to react.

He grabbed her face, his large hand gripping each side of her jaw in an unforgiving hold. Marcie winced as he squeezed, forcing her head up and her eyes to look into his. She tried not to let her fear show, but she was practically trembling with it. He must have only woken up within the last few minutes. What on earth could have happened to provoke this kind of behavior?

"Tanner, what the hell is wrong with you? Get your hands off me!"

"You fuck those guys?" he asked between clenched teeth.

That's what this was about? Hook and Striker? He'd obviously lost his mind. Maybe some kind of alcohol-induced psychosis. "What? Tanner are you crazy? I talked to them for five minutes. When would I have done that?"

"I don't mean last night, bitch, I mean when you lived here. You fuck one of them? Both of them? Maybe at the same time?" The staid lawyer was unrecognizable with his eyes hangover-bloodshot and his mouth twisted in an angry snarl. Around her jaw, his long fingers tightened with each question.

"No! God, Tanner, I was sixteen when I left here." Marcie pulled her head back, trying to dislodge her jaw from his strong grasp.

"Do you have any idea how stupid you made me look?" Spittle landed on her cheeks.

"What do you mean? I was just talking to friends I haven't seen in ten years." Tears filled her eyes as his hold tightened to bruising.

"You were draped all over that one asshole like a slut. It makes me look like a pussy who can't control his woman. I won't tolerate it, Marcie." His voice continued to rise and his dark eyes were full of threatening promises.

Who was this man? Yes, Tanner had proven to be self-centered, egotistical, and thoughtless over the past few days, but this enraged, jealous maniac was someone she hadn't encountered before. How was she supposed to handle this belligerence?

"I grew up with them, Tanner, they were just friends. We were kids." The expression *lights on nobody's home* flashed through her mind as she watched him. It was like her words didn't register in his rage-soaked brain.

Just as he opened his mouth, there was a sharp knock on the motel room door. Awareness finally filtered into Tanner's gaze. He blinked and stared at his hand on her face as though it wasn't under his control. "Oh my God, Marcie. I'm so sorry." His fingers freed her sore face.

"Come on you lovebirds," Billy shouted from the other side of the door. "Can you two stop going at it so we can grab some breakfast? We're starved." His *we* referred to Cameron, the other friend Tanner had invited along on the trip to bury her mother.

"We'll uh, we'll be out in a minute, dude," Tanner called back. He kept his attention on her. "Marcie, I don't know what happened. Please forgi—"

She held up a trembling hand. Forgiveness was great and all, but this was too much. "Look, Tanner. This seems very out of character for you, so let's chalk it up to a momentary lapse of judgment." Not that she really believed his personality would make a crazy shift just once. But she wanted out of this bathroom without another scene. "I was thinking it would be better to wait until we got home to do this, but now I think it's just best to get it out of the way. I'm not sure we're right for each other, and I think we should probably stop dating." There, she said it. Easy, unemotional, and hopefully well received.

His hands dropped to his sides and he bowed his head in defeat. "I get it. I scared you."

He sure as hell had. "It's more than just that. The connection just isn't there for me. I'm sorry, I hope you understand."

"I do. And, again, I'm really sorry for this. Um…don't waste your money on a plane ticket. Let's just get some food and drive back home. I'll respect your space and your decision."

This was the calm, rational Tanner she'd known for the last two weeks. Not that it fooled her. Something darker lurked under the mild-mannered exterior. But a last-minute plane ticket was the last thing she wanted to pay for. "Okay. That sounds fair. I'll meet you outside."

He left and Marcie shut the bathroom door and threw on a pair of denim cutoffs with an eggplant ribbed tank top. She glanced in the mirror.

Damnit. Faint purple marks lined her jaw. Her hands trembled as she dug through her toiletry bag. They couldn't get to Seattle fast enough. She wanted her apartment, and her bed, and the tub of fudge brownie ice cream waiting in her freezer.

Without much finesse, she slapped some cover-up on her face. She turned her head from side to side. Good enough. It looked like she had a bit too much makeup on, but at least the bruises were hidden. Not so much for the ones on her arms, but anything with sleeves was already in the suitcase in the car.

After slipping her feet in jeweled flip-flops, she exited the bathroom and headed out after the guys in the parking lot.

When she reached Tanner's black Audi Q7 SUV, his pride and joy, she was greeted by frustrated male cursing. Ugh, what now? Five seconds ago, he was fine. This new bout of anger better not have anything to do with her.

"I can't fucking believe it! Fifty thousand dollars for this fucking car and the piece of shit won't start. It's five months old! Where the fuck is Marcie?"

She bit her lip to keep from smirking at Tanner's dismay. He used that car as a status symbol and bragged about it endlessly. The car was unnecessary, especially since the one he traded in was only a year and a half old. Ninety percent of the time, he drove the two miles from his condo to his office. What the hell did he need a luxury vehicle for? She couldn't help but take some smug pleasure in his predicament. "I'm right here, Tanner."

"Where's the closest Audi dealer?"

Without thinking, Marcie burst out laughing. "Out here? Probably two plus hours away."

"Damnit, this is the shittiest town ever." He wound up with his leg and threw a vicious kick at the rear tire. A loud curse broke through the morning silence as his foot collided with the tire.

Tanner's friends both stared at fascinating spots on the asphalt. Of course, they wouldn't get involved. Come to think of it, neither looked very surprised by his outburst. Was this his typical behavior? If so, he'd managed to hide it well for a few weeks. "We are a bit off the grid here. There won't be a dealership for a few hundred miles, but there is a garage in town."

"I'm supposed to let some backward desert hick work on my car?" He snorted. "I don't think so." He ran a hand through his impeccable hair, scattering the strands in multiple directions.

Marcie didn't bother to let him know, again taking a bit of guilty pleasure in seeing him out of sorts. "I don't see that you have any other options right now."

"It'll be fine, man." Billy rubbed a hand over his buzz-cut and rolled his eyes. He'd been in the military and hadn't lost the haircut or the muscles in the few years since he'd been discharged.

"Yeah, let's just call a tow. You and Marcie can ride to the garage with them. Billy and I will grab a cab, get some grub, and meet up with you at the garage." Cam looked between Tanner and Marcie. His fire-engine-red hair shone in the sun. The guy should probably find some shade before his freckled skin roasted.

Tanner grunted. "Fine. Marcie, make the call."

Marcie bristled at the command in his tone, but all she wanted was to get the hell out of there. It would be all over as soon as they got to Seattle. Turning away, she fished her phone out of her purse. She dialed four-one-one and held the cellphone to her ear.

"Information, how may I assist you today?" A clear crisp voice greeted her.

"Good morning. I need a number for a tow truck in Crystal Rock, Arizona."

"Certainly, please hold one moment while I retrieve that for you."

As Marcie waited, Tanner trudged around the parking lot, one stomp away from a full-blown temper tantrum. Billy stood by trying to calm him while Cameron paced, off to the side, on his own phone, probably calling for a taxi.

"Okay, ma'am, the tow truck comes from the NP Garage and the number is..." As the operator rattled off the ten digits, Marcie had to force herself to pay attention. How could she have forgotten that the garage was adjacent to the No Prisoners' clubhouse?

Shit.

Now she'd have to accompany Tanner onto their turf. Lifting her eyes heavenward, she sent up a little prayer asking that Hook and Striker not be there today. Though if she was honest, the thought of seeing Hook again sent a thrill zinging through her blood.

After she disconnected with information, she placed a call to the garage, and strolled back over to where the men were waiting. "They'll be here in ten minutes." No point in telling Tanner who owned the garage; it would be apparent soon enough.

Just a few minutes later a taxi rolled into the motel parking lot.

"Okay, we'll go pick up some food from that diner we saw yesterday, then have the cab drop us off at the garage. Anything specific you guys want?" Cam asked.

"Um, you know what? I'll get the food, you guys go to the garage." Thank you, Cam, for giving her an out. She moved toward the cab but Cameron waved her off.

"No need, girl. Stay with your man." He winked.

Ugh, this really wasn't the time to announce their breakup to the guys, with an open taxi door and curious driver looking on. Looked like she'd be hanging with Tanner for a few minutes. Hopefully, she could refrain from slapping him if he opened his mouth again.

Cam and Billy filed into the classic-looking yellow taxi. The taillights receded and she was once again alone with Tanner. Her heart rate kicked up a notch. Would he go off on her again?

Thankfully, as the cab turned out onto the highway, a tow truck rumbled into the parking lot. Marcie waved, catching the attention of the driver as he slowed and rolled the truck into position behind Tanner's SUV.

A thin man with shaggy blond hair that curled around his ears climbed out of the cab. He had to be at least six foot four, with long spindly arms and legs. Marcie bit back a chuckle as she had the thought that the man looked rubbery, as though someone had stretched him out and he hadn't yet shrunk back.

Thick, dark, rectangular glasses sat on his face, reminding her more of a geeky college professor than an outlaw motorcycle club member. But he wore the identifying No Prisoners cut, confirming he was in fact a patched member of the club.

"Fancy ride." The stretched-out man didn't bother to introduce himself. "You called about a tow, right?" He looked at Marcie.

She opened her mouth, but Tanner beat her to it, holding out a hand to the newcomer. "Hey, buddy, I'm Tanner." He pointed to the car. "She won't start, won't even turn over. Bitches, right?"

The lanky man ignored Tanner's attempt at male posturing, and raised one brow, turning toward Marcie.

The heat of embarrassment rushed to her face, first because Tanner had only introduced himself, leaving her standing next to him like a statue. And secondly, because of his demeaning, sophomoric joke.

"Hey there, darlin', the name's Gumby. You the one who called?"

She never would have come up with it, but Gumby was a perfect nickname for the gangly man. Marcie was able to swallow the laugh that threatened, but she couldn't keep the grin off her face.

"I know, girl, believe me I know." He seemed to guess where her thoughts had taken her.

She reached out, placing her hand in his much larger one. "Marcie, and yes I called you."

"Okay then." He released her hand and walked with extra-long strides toward the tow truck. "You guys can hop on in. Air's running. I'll have this baby loaded up in no time. Garage is about ten minutes from here, and we should be able to check it out right away."

When he reached the passenger side door, he wrenched it open. With an exaggerated flourish of his lengthy arm, he gestured into the vehicle. "Ladies first."

Charmed, Marcie smiled and started for the truck, but the smile was short lived as she snuck a glance in Tanner's direction. His face was a mask of anger, yet again. Why was he acting so jealous and possessive? She'd just broken up with him for crying out loud.

The interior of the truck was blessedly cool, as the day had already begun to significantly heat up. Marcie slid to the center and gazed through the windshield, not surprised to see Tanner hadn't budged.

"Coming man? We're letting all the lady's cool air escape," Gumby said.

"I'll supervise you hooking up my car."

Marcie rolled her eyes. Tanner's use of the word *supervise* was purposeful, as though Gumby couldn't do his job and needed Tanner to oversee the process. He could barely find the gas tank; there was no way he'd know how to rig up a tow.

She enjoyed a few minutes of peace in the cool, quiet truck before the doors opened simultaneously and each man slid in. Sitting sandwiched between the two men was slightly awkward, but she didn't really have another option.

Gumby put the truck in gear, checked the mirror, and drove toward the exit. "So darlin', rumor has it you grew up around these parts."

He had a bit of a southern twang, and Marcie took a second to wonder where he was from.

Tanner stiffened. "How the fuck do you know that?" Tanner's voice snapped through the car.

Hook

Well, Tanner seemed to have given up on feeble his attempt to be chummy with Gumby, and was now resorting back to straight up jerk. Fantastic.

"Hey," she whispered. "Tone it down."

Gumby directed his attention toward Marcie. "Hook overheard you call in and gave me a heads up. Told me to give you the royal treatment."

"Who the fuck is Hook?"

Okay, she'd had enough of his childish attitude. The look she gave him would have boiled water.

Gumby continued as though Tanner hadn't uttered a word. "In fact, I think Hook's exact words were something like, 'Treat her like family. Hit on her and I'll rip your nuts off.'" He mimicked Hook's accent and laughed. "I thought that was interesting." He winked.

Marcie let out a shaky chuckle.

"Oh, please." Tanner rolled his eyes.

"Hey, man, relax. You don't want to go in there swinging your dick around. I'm laid back and easy going. Some of these guys —" He snorted. "Just lose the attitude."

Marcie had a feeling Gumby could be anything but calm and easygoing if the situation called for it. He may look like a lanky college professor, but he was still an outlaw biker. They weren't known for laid back or easygoing.

Gumby slowed the tow truck to a stop outside the garage. Before the vehicle was in park, Tanner shoved the door open and hopped down. He slammed the door behind him, leaving Marcie and Gumby still sitting in the icy cab.

"I'm so sorry." She shook her head. Despite the chill of the truck, the heat of embarrassment had sweat rolling down her spine. Tanner stomped through the parking lot in the opposite direction of the garage. Hopefully a quick walk would clear his head and cool him off. As much as a hundred-degree day could cool anyone down.

"Ain't on you, darlin'. Hook told me the guy seemed like a bit of a wank. I couldn't help but poke him a little. I should be the one apologizing." He opened his door and stepped out, his long legs easily reaching the ground. Once again, he held the door for her, and the gesture charmed her. "Come on, darlin'. I know your guys are excited to see you again."

She scooted along the seat and climbed down from the truck, taking the hand Gumby offered for support. "Thanks." Heat accosted her as she followed him into the large, open garage, which was adjacent to the clubhouse.

Four open garage bays lined the long building, allowing the men to communicate with each other while working. One other car was up on a jack in the first bay, and there were a number of motorcycles in various states of assembly. Some appeared really old and beat up to Marcie's uneducated eye, while others were amazing, looking more like works of art than something you'd ride through the dusty desert roads. One in particular caught her eye. A shiny, polished bike, with an intricate design on the gas tank.

"Gorgeous, huh?" Gumby asked.

"I know absolutely nothing about motorcycles, but even I can appreciate the sophisticated detail work that must have gone into that."

"That's Striker, Hook, and Jester for you. They do custom builds and renovations, best work in the west."

Impressed, Marcie sniffed and the pungent smell of motor oil tickled her senses. There was a low level of chatter from some men working on car and every now and again, a loud clank rang out as a tool connected with some portion of a vehicle. She ran her hand over the cool leather of the seat. "Must be difficult to part with it after all that work."

"It can be, babe," Striker said from behind her.

Marcie spun, and as he hugged her, a warm feeling of belonging bloomed in her chest.

"Sucks that your car crapped out on you, but I'm glad to see you again before you skip town."

"Me too." As she returned Striker's affectionate hug, Marcie noticed Hook staring at her from about ten feet away. His gaze was dark, intense, and if she wasn't mistaken, honed in on the three round purple bruises that decorated her upper arm.

Shit!

She'd expected nothing more than a day of driving and hadn't thought to go back and cover up the marks after the car died. After she released Striker, she attempted to conceal the bruising by turning her body so her right arm was no longer in Hook's line of sight.

He sidled on up to her and Striker. "What's up with the car?"

Marcie cleared her throat as nervous butterflies flitted low in her stomach. Hook's focus was still trained on her, like a caress against her skin. Her nipples hardened against the thin fabric of her tank top.

Oh God. Had Hook noticed?

A muscle ticked in his jaw as his eyes shifted downward a fraction. He noticed. The shift was subtle, and Marcie was probably the only one aware of it, but it had a devastating effect on her. Her panties flooded and she unconsciously adjusted her position. A slow grin crept across Hook's handsome face.

There was no way he could know she was wet, was there?

Marcie scrambled for an escape from Hook's penetrating stare. "It, uh, it won't start. Totally dead." She shifted her stance.

Tanner strode into the garage, his heavy tread indicating his continued displeasure.

"I'm not sure beyond that." Marcie winced at the husky nature of her voice. She cleared her throat. "You'll have to ask Tanner. Can you tell me where the restroom is?"

"Sure, hon, it's in the lobby, at the end of the hallway to the left after the reception desk." Striker pointed to the left side of the garage.

Marcie spun and scurried off, sure that Hook was fully aware of her cowardly getaway plan.

CHAPTER FIVE

Hook suppressed an amused grin as Marcie turned tail and escaped to the privacy of the restroom, her hips swaying with each quick step. He'd stared at her as though he wanted to devour every inch of her sexy body, which was pretty accurate to his actual desire since he laid eyes on her in the bar.

The majority of the previous night had been spent tossing and turning, hard as a fuckin' stone, while thoughts of Marcie riding his cock flashed through his mind. Along with thoughts of Marcie sucking him off. And thoughts of Marcie moaning while he buried his face between her smooth thighs. Some alone time in the shower had taken care of the hard-on, but hadn't done anything to dampen the desire eating at him since she walked back into his life.

He wanted her. Plain and simple. Hook had his share of female companions. Hell, all his MC brothers did. Something about the leather and motorcycles. Maybe even the fact that they danced over the line of the law more often than not. Bad boys drew women like flies to honey.

Thoughts of honey had him imaging how sweet Marcie would taste. He'd wanted her ten years ago, when she was far too young to do anything about it. In her absence, he'd managed to bury the attraction and feelings that had always been more than just physical desire. He was older now, smarter, harder. And so was she. She wasn't an innocent sixteen-year-old. She was a woman and he wasn't sure he was willing to let her walk out of his life a second time.

Tanner must have picked up on Hook's poorly hidden interest because the stay-away-from-my-woman vibes rolling off the man were difficult to miss. He glared at Hook, eyes narrowed, posture tense as if he thought himself intimidating.

Please. If the pissing contest came to blows, Hook was one hundred and ten percent confident he'd have the prick laid out and crying in under fifteen seconds.

Unfortunately for Tanner, Hook was used to going after and getting what he wanted when it came to the fairer sex. About halfway through the night, he decided that he wanted Marcie and was going to have her. Normally not one to poach another man's property, Hook justified it by telling himself Marcie didn't seem happy with this bastard. And he was a bastard.

The purple circular bruises on Marcie's arm were clearly made by a man's fingers squeezing her fragile skin. No way in hell had he put them there himself when he held her arm. He'd sooner run his bike off a cliff. That left Tanner. For that alone, he'd gladly steal Marcie away, and wouldn't write off putting a couple marks on the little shit as well.

"What's up with the car, Tanner?" Striker asked, oblivious to the storm brewing between the two other men.

"Piece of shit's only five months old and it just won't start." He shook his head in disgust.

"Okay, I'll have someone take a look at it right now. Come with me." He motioned for Tanner to follow him deeper into the garage where they could fill out some intake paperwork.

Hook took advantage of the solitary moment to wander into the lobby.

Karen, their President Shiv's ol' lady, sat behind the desk, on the phone with a client. She split the hours as receptionist with Jazmine, a spunky biker chick with hot pink hair and multiple piercings who'd been working for them a few months. Focused on her call, Karen gave Hook an absent wave without glancing away from the computer.

He slipped past her. With a quick-as-lightning motion, he reached down and pilfered the key to the single stall bathroom from a box on the desk. Normally the door wasn't locked, but with Marcie in there it would be. Oblivious, Karen plugged away at the computer while she chatted with the client.

Victory. Hook crept down the hallway and slid the key in the lock, unable to keep a grin of anticipation off his face.

The door swung in and Marcie, who was standing at the sink drying her hands with a stiff paper towel, jolted. "Hook," she said, her voice nearly a shriek. Her hand flew to her chest, as though trying to hold her racing heart in place. "Jesus, you scared me. I locked the door. How did you get in here?"

He held out his hand, dangling the key from his pinky finger.

Marcie chuckled, the sound shaky and a bit unsure. She crumpled the paper towel back and forth between her hands. "You make a habit of barging in on women in the bathroom?"

Hook's eyes were drawn to the bruising on her arm like a magnet. Displeasure filled him, warring with the desire she evoked. Still silent, he pulled the paper from her hands and tossed it in the trash.

Close enough to smell the sweet fragrance wafting off her golden hair; he gently wrapped a hand around her arm, right above her elbow. He held it in place as he examined the angry marks. Tanner would pay for this. It wasn't a question. The man would not leave town until he understood that marking Marcie was unacceptable.

At least marking her in anger. Hook's cock swelled at the thought of leaving a few signs of pleasure on her incredible body.

Marcie couldn't breathe. Her heart raced and blood pounded in her ears, but not in fear. Not like it had this morning, in another bathroom, with a different man equally close. Hook's gentle touch set off a shock wave of longing. Both physical and emotional. The tender way he caressed the sore skin of her arm made her want to weep.

Accompanied by his touch was an intense feeling of homecoming, belonging, acceptance, and a strong dose of desire. With each light stroke of his strong finger, ripples of electricity travelled up her arm, finding their way to her aching nipples.

Mesmerized, she watched his handsome face cloud over as he inspected her. Clearly, he'd figured out where the bruising came from. Part of Marcie was embarrassed, not wanting him to see her as any kind of victim or weak female while the other part reveled in his singular attentiveness. "I'm fine, Hook," she whispered, the intimacy of the moment seeming to demand quietly spoken words.

Hook maintained his silence as he bent his head, replacing his wandering finger with the gentle brush of his full lips. A lump of emotion formed in Marcie's throat and grew thicker with each soft kiss on her flesh. Her eyelids drifted down and pleasure coursed through her. She wasn't sure what the hell was happening, but it was too good to question.

Hook drew back and Marcie felt the acute loss of his affection. With a contented sigh, she let her eyes flutter open, and found herself staring into the depths of Hook's deep brown eyes. Desire and lust smoldered in his gaze, promising her she wasn't the only one affected by the chemistry sizzling between them.

Marcie's brain screamed at her to stop, stop reaching for this man she once knew, but was a stranger to her now. This older version was stronger, sexier, and more dangerous than the boy she'd grown up with. It would be so easy to fall into him, let him hold her, pleasure her, comfort her. But when it was over, she'd still be alone, and a little weaker for having let him shoulder some of her burdens. Then the next time she needed to be tough and stand on her own, she'd remember what it felt like to have Hook, and it would be just a bit harder to go on alone.

But the temptation was there. And it was like the mighty pull of a powerful magnet. Possibly stronger than she could resist.

Her hands connected with his chest, fisting the soft material of his worn gray T-shirt, and dragged his body against her own. The feel of his muscular frame making contact with her, even through layers of clothing, was enough to ignite the incendiary passion that had been simmering since she'd seen him last night.

Hook's mouth descended and all rational thoughts fled. He fused his lips to hers in a kiss so hot, so intense, her knees wobbled. Need like she'd never known coursed through her and were it not for Hook walking her backward until she connected with the side of the bathroom stall, trapping her against it, she would have slid to a boneless puddle on the floor.

Hook devoured her mouth, sweeping his tongue inside to duel with hers. He raked her bottom lip between his teeth before trailing a path of fiery kisses along the sensitive skin of her jaw. Marcie lifted one leg, securing it around his trim hips and shamelessly tilted her pelvis, looking for some friction to ease the consuming ache that had developed between her legs.

She moaned as his mouth met the spot where her neck dipped to her shoulder. He bit down lightly on the taut tendon, then soothed the sting with his tongue. At the same time, his hands slid down her back, palming her ass and holding her even closer, directly against his erection.

Ripples of pleasure shot from everywhere Hook touched, overloading her brain with endorphins. Moisture pooled between her legs and her pussy clenched as though protesting its vacant state. Could Hook sense it? Did he know she was more aroused by his kiss and over-the-clothes petting than she'd ever been in her life? She wanted him inside her. If he could make her burn with just one kiss, their joining would be explosive.

"Hook? Where the fuck are you, bro? Striker needs you to order a part for the Audi." A thunderous voice rang out from the lobby and the spell was broken.

Chest heaving, Marcie tried to unwind her leg from around his hips, but he still held her ass, rocking her pelvis firmly against his arousal. She stared at him wide-eyed, a bit embarrassed by her uninhibited behavior.

"There's no fucking way you have this with him," Hook whispered, his voice strained, like he was struggling to control himself as he referenced her relationship with Tanner. He inhaled a slow, deep breath. "Christ, Marcie, I can fucking feel how much you want me. You're hot as hell, even through your clothes."

"Oh my God." Mortified, Marcie pushed against his chest. Time to dislodge herself before she died of humiliation.

He tightened his grip and prevented her escape. "No way, baby. Don't you dare be ashamed. It's fuckin' hot."

"I can't believe...I mean I've never..." How to explain this brazen behavior? But Hook didn't seem to be listening. His gaze had shifted a little lower, focused on her neck.

"What's wrong?" She drew one hand up to her neck.

Finally releasing her bottom, Hook smoothed one finger over the junction between her shoulder and neck. "I left my mark on you," he said with a smug grin.

"What!" Marcie was still whispering but the sound had become desperate. She wiggled her hips and brought her leg back down ignoring Hook's groan of frustration as she bumped against his still hard cock and turned toward the mirror. Sure enough, a small maroon spot marred her skin. "Everyone will see!" She couldn't keep the worry from her voice.

Hook moved in behind her, ran his hands up her sides, and placed a soothing kiss over the mark.

"Oh no you don't." Over her shoulder, Marcie smacked the center of his forehead and shoved him off her neck.

With a soft laugh, he slid a finger under the strap of her tank top and lifted, moving it ever so slightly to the right, directly over the love bite. "There, now you and I are the only ones who will know." His eyes held a mischievous glow.

"Hook! What the fuck, man?" A pounding on the door had Marcie jumping out of her skin.

"I'm coming, dickhead!" Hook responded before turning his attention back to Marcie. "We both would have been if I'd had five more minutes." He winked. "I'll go out first, wait one minute until I get Jester out of the lobby then you can follow."

Marcie nodded her approval. Hook spun her around and gave her a quick kiss before pivoting on his heel and heading toward the door.

"Hook, wait." The words flew out of her mouth without her brain's consent.

He turned and raised a brow in question.

"It's never been like that." She swallowed and held his gaze. She wasn't one to put her emotional cards on the table, but in for a penny, in for a pound. "With him. And it's over. I told him this morning. He was..." She rubbed a hand over the abused skin of her arm. "Well, it's just over."

Hook dipped his chin once, a triumphant smile on his face. "Good to know." He winked and slipped out to the lobby.

Marcie smiled and fanned herself, her eyes riveted to his tight ass flexing against the denim as he walked. Her head spun with the events of the past fifteen hours. Feelings she'd locked away in a vault the day she moved, rushed her like a linebacker. She'd missed it here. Maybe she'd just missed Hook and Striker. Maybe she'd sacrificed something by becoming so self-sufficient. Connections, relationships.

No. That wasn't it.

It was something much more basic. Pheromones, hormones, lust. That's all it was. Her resolve was stronger than her baser desires. She could overcome it. All she needed to do was remember what life was like when she knew Hook and Striker. How she'd been a helpless little girl who needed others to protect her, help her, take care of her. She didn't need any of that now. Hook might look like the pot of gold at the end of a rainbow, but he didn't fit into the new life she'd created for herself.

She was strong. She could triumph over a fierce attraction to a man...maybe.

CHAPTER SIX

Hook ran through the garage's tool inventory as he emerged from the bathroom. All his mental faculties went toward willing his erection to go down before he reached the end of the hallway and encountered an impatiently waiting Jester. Luckily, it seemed to work and he was decent by the time his oversized friend spotted him entering the reception area.

"Jesus, bro, I was about to tell Shiv to charge you rent. Everything okay in there?" Jester patted his stomach in case Hook didn't pick up on his meaning. His customary smirk was plastered on his face. The man wasn't happy unless he was busting someone's balls.

"Mind your own fucking business. Let's move." Hook wanted the other man back in the garage bay before Marcie appeared. If Jester witnessed her slink from the restroom, the shit he'd give Hook would be fierce and endless.

"You put your panties on backward in there or something? Give me a minute, I need to look up a fax number." His size fourteen feet tromped to the now-vacant reception desk.

Shit. As Jester moved behind the wooden desk to the computer, Hook's mind raced to come up with a fast way to get him out of there. Unfortunately, Marcie chose that moment to emerge from the hallway, stopping short when she noticed the two men lingering around the reception desk.

"Oh, um...I—" she stammered, gaze darting in every direction but at Hook.

He watched, amused as her gaze landed on Jester and those gorgeous green eyes widened in shock. Jester tended to have that effect on initial impression. A hulk of a man, he was nearly six and a half feet tall, with an overabundance of muscles. Hook was one of the few people who knew Jester was an avid weight lifter. For some reason, the man was shy about that piece of information. His left arm had a sleeve of tattoos, and he'd recently started on the right. Typically, he wore his long dark hair tied back at the nape of his neck.

The bodybuilder physique combined with the extreme height and yards of ink made for one intimidating picture. His constant joking and sarcasm always surprised people, both of which were how his name came about.

If Marcie's reaction to Jester was predictable, his reaction to her was cliché. She was undeniably a knockout and Jester loved women, particularly gorgeous ones. He pushed back the rolling office chair that groaned under his substantial weight and smiled a toothy grin full of mirth. "Ohh, now I get it." He jumped up and made his way toward Marcie.

"Jester." Hook's voice held a note of warning.

"Hello, beautiful. You must be the Marcie this one hasn't shut up about since last night," Jester said, motioning a thumb in Hook's direction.

A delightful shade of pink rose from her neck to her cheeks. "Oh, um, well yes, I'm Marcie." As she spoke, her eyes darted toward the exit. There was a good chance she'd disappear if he blinked too long.

The shit-eating grin returned to Jester's face and he slid his thumbs through the belt loops on his pants, rocking back on his heels. "Sooo, Hook's zipper get stuck?"

Marcie gasped and sputtered. "I-I'm sorry, what?"

"That's why you were in the bathroom, right? I assume he was taking a leak and must have gotten his zipper stuck, so he called for help. You happened to be walking by and came to his rescue. What other explanation could there be?"

Hook couldn't keep the growl of frustration inside. On a normal day, he tried not to let Jester's ribbing get under his skin, but he'd be taking his brother out back for an ass beating if he kept flustering her, Jester's size be damned. But, as usual with Jester's teasing nature, he charmed a chuckle out of Marcie.

"Actually, no. Somehow, he locked himself in the stall and needed someone to help him climb out."

Jester threw back his head and laughed, a booming sound that had Marcie's eyes widening once again. "Not bad, girlie. And might I add, you are every bit as gorgeous as Hook told me you were."

The grin that had graced Hook's face at Marcie's wit faded with Jester's comment. Teasing was bad enough. No way he'd tolerate full frontal flirting. "Okay, asshole, don't you have some shit to do?" Hook served as manager for the garage and was in charge of all the men during working hours.

"Yeah, yeah. I'm getting there, boss. FYI the part we need for your boyfriend's Audi won't get here until tomorrow." He stressed the word boyfriend and glanced toward Marcie. "Looks like you're stuck in Crystal Rock for one more night."

Hook couldn't discern whether Marcie was horrified or elated by that news. Her gaze darted between them as though searching for something to say when Jester jumped to her rescue. "I think Tanner called you guys a cab and his buddy is here with some food. Said you were pretty hungry."

Marcie's eyes lit up at the mention of breakfast. "Yes! I'm famished, thank you…"

"Jester, darlin'." He held out a massive mitt and engulfed Marcie's smaller hand. He brought it up toward his mouth for a polite kiss.

It was quite obvious Jester was trying to get under his skin, trying to get him to show his cards and act like a possessive ape. He didn't give a shit that he was playing right into his brother's hand. "When you're done drooling over our client, get your ass back to work."

Jester just laughed and shot Marcie a wink as he exited through the door leading directly into the garage.

"Come on, babe, let's get you outside before someone puts an APB out on you." Hook moved toward the door and pulled it toward him, allowing Marcie to precede him through the exit. Four sets of male eyes trained on them when they strolled through the parking lot. Striker was in the lot talking with an unimpressed looking Tanner and his two buddies who seemed mildly embarrassed by Tanner's moody attitude. One of the men tossed a foil wrapped breakfast sandwich to Marcie and she unwrapped it and dug right in with a moan of pleasure.

The small sound had Hook rising to half-mast once again. The idea of her driving out of town caused an uncomfortable ache on the left side of his chest. He needed an excuse to see her again. Hell, maybe he'd just show up at her motel room and demand she go out with him. Her impending departure loomed ahead like a ticking time bomb. Who was he kidding? One date wouldn't be nearly enough. Now that she was back in his life, he wanted time with her. Wanted to see what could develop between them. Wanted to spend days on end in bed with her.

Striker slung an arm around her shoulders and drew her to his side. Tanner tensed and his nostrils flared like a pissed off bull. "Hey, Marce, I was planning to go to Hook's this evening to grill some steaks. You should join us since you're stuck here another night. It will give us more time to catch up."

God, sometimes he really loved Striker.

Marcie's face lit with pleasure at the suggestion. "Oh, I would love to." The light in her eyes dimmed a fraction. "Do you guys care if I abandon you?"

Tanner let out a snort and rolled his eyes, but one of his buddies shook his head. "Nah, we can entertain ourselves. Have fun catching up with your friends." The guy cast a sideways look at Tanner as though uncertain of his friend's response, but

Hook

Tanner managed to control himself beyond a ticking jaw and narrowed glare.

"Let me give you my address. Take your phone out, Marce." The nickname slipped out, but he couldn't deny how much he enjoyed Tanner's clenched teeth when he heard it. When she had the phone in her hands, he rattled off where he lived.

"Great." Marcie's smile returned, and she keyed the address in her phone. "Umm, Hook? Can you cook?" She asked, eyes sparkling.

"Excuse me," he scoffed.

Striker shook his head and mouthed, "No fucking way."

"Baby, I can grill one hell of a steak and that's all you need to worry about." He enjoyed the pretty pink blush that flushed her face.

Tanner, as usual, looked like he'd sucked a lemon, but Hook didn't give a flying fuck what the other man thought. Hadn't Marcie said she ended it with him? Guess the guy wasn't too happy about her decision. Not that Hook could blame him. She was a prize and he sure as hell wouldn't give her up without a fight.

"Ok then. I'll bring something sweet for desert." Marcie winked, unseen by Tanner as she'd turned away from him.

Her flirty comment wasn't lost on Tanner, though, and his face twisted into even more of a grimace.

Hook had a fleeting moment of worry for Marcie who would be spending the rest of the afternoon with the pissed off man, but surely Tanner wouldn't be stupid enough to pull something when Hook and Striker would be seeing her soon.

Striker had presented him with the perfect opportunity to have some alone time with Marcie. Now he just had to use the gift wisely. He was on it like grease on an engine.

CHAPTER SEVEN

At six forty-five, Marcie stood outside her motel room in the sweltering evening heat waiting for the cab to arrive, a bakery box tucked under one arm. She hadn't spoken to Tanner since the taxi dropped them off at the motel hours earlier and he'd stormed off. Hook had the presence of mind to ask if she needed anything from the car before she left the garage, which prompted her to remember her suitcase in the trunk. She'd wheeled the bag straight to the front office of the motel. Thankfully, they had a few vacancies and she was able to procure a room of her own. The unintended expense would suck, but she also looked into purchasing a last-minute plane ticket. No way was she spending the next few days trapped in a car with Tanner.

Spending time with Hook and Striker this evening would be great; even better if some of that time ended up as Hook-only time. All afternoon, she'd replayed the stolen moments in the bathroom with him until she was so turned on she'd had no choice but to do something about it. She'd lain on the cheap motel linens and fingered herself until she came, hard, Hook's name flying from her mouth. Unfortunately, instead of being sated, all she could think about was how much better it would feel if it were Hook's fingers inside her, or his tongue, or his cock.

Jesus, she needed to get her libido under control. Technically, she was now single, but she wasn't the type to hop from one bed to another. Although, Hook might be a temptation far too delicious to resist.

While she was still waiting on her cab, Tanner stumbled around the side of the building, with the bleary-eyed look of someone who'd had one—or six—too many drinks. Well, shit. This was not going to be good.

He seemed to be staggering his way straight toward her, so she steeled herself for an unpleasant encounter. The taxi would arrive any second. At least that gave her a quick out.

"Hey, hon," he greeted her as he sidled up to her. Bending down, Tanner landed an open-mouth kiss on her shoulder.

"What the hell? Get off me." She gently pushed him off and took three sizable steps back.

"I missed you all afternoon," he said as he moved closer. "I thought maybe you'd like it if I came with you to your friend's house."

She shook her head. Just how many personalities did the man have? "No, Tanner. I wouldn't like that. You crossed way over the line this morning into abusive. And I told you we were finished. You need to go sleep it off in your room for a few hours."

He advanced on her until he was close enough she could count the bloodshot lines in his eyes.

"Come on, honey, don't be like that." An arm snaked around her and he nuzzled his nose into the crook of her neck. His other hand slid up her stomach and cupped a breast.

Every cell in her body stiffened. She was about two seconds away from grabbing his balls and twisting with all her might. "Tanner, if you ever want the option of having children, you'll get your fucking hands off me, right now. I told you this morning we were finished, and I meant it."

"Don't think I can't see what you're doing." Tanner snarled and plastered himself against her. "You want to end this so you can fuck those dirty bikers."

Well, he was partially right. She sure as hell wanted Hook, but that fact had nothing to do with the end of their disastrous relationship.

She tried to nudge him back, but his hold was surprisingly strong. "No, Tanner, I don't *want* it to end. I ended it already. This morning. There isn't anything left to end. Now back the hell off. I have no idea what you think you're going to accomplish here. There is no way you're coming with me. I don't want you there, and Striker and Hook will not tolerate your presence." As the words left her mouth, a huge sense of peace and relief wrapped around her like a soft blanket.

Dammit. There she went, throwing their names around like they were her personal bodyguards. Using them to solve problems she needed to handle on her own. And there was the problem with spending any time with Hook. It was just far too easy to forget the importance of independence. Against all her self-reliant instincts, the idea of Striker and Hook waiting for her, supporting her, provided a sense of calm that was immediate and strong.

It lasted all of about twenty seconds.

With a too-firm stroke, Tanner slid his hand up her back and fisted it in her hair. He gripped the short strands tight and twisted his wrist until the taut wrench brought tears to her eyes. Marcie's heart leaped to her throat and the bakery box dropped to the ground. She might be independent, but she had zero skills as far as self-defense. A mistake. She'd be enrolling in a class the second she returned home.

"Tanner, please," she said, fear ratcheting up her anxiety with each passing second. She was completely immobile. Any movement only increased the pain of his grip on her hair. She felt the pop as strands were uprooted from her scalp.

"There's something you need to understand, bitch," he whispered against her ear. "This is over when *I* say it's over. You think I'm going to walk away so you can go fuck one of those grease monkeys from the garage?" He snorted. "Think again, honey. Here's what's gonna happen."

His hot breath reeked of stale liquor and Marcie breathed through her mouth to avoid the nauseating stench.

The rumble of a vehicle rolling into the lot diverted Tanner's attention and he loosened his hold on her hair. Marcie rammed her elbow into his stomach. Thankfully, the impulsive move had him grunting and he released her.

She drew her phone from her rear pocket and held it out as though brandishing a weapon. "Stay the hell away from me. If you try to get in this cab I will call the cops and you can spend the night in the town lock-up instead of your hotel room. It's over, Tanner. Done. This is the last we'll talk about it."

She retrieved the box of sweet treats and walked backward away from Tanner, reluctant to take her focus off him.

The cab pulled up to the curb and Marcie turned her attention away from Tanner. One quick peek over her shoulder as she slid into the seat proved he was smart enough to take her threat of calling the cops seriously.

Heart pounding, she rattled the address off to the pleasant, balding driver. As he hit the gas and drove onto the road, she blew out a giant breath. The eight-minute drive was spent in silence, and was just enough time to get her erratic breathing and hammering pulse under control.

"That will be ten dollars, miss," the driver said as he coasted to a stop in front of the requested address.

She dropped a ten and a five into his open palm. "Thank you. Keep the change."

"Thank you, miss. You have yourself a good evening."

That was the plan. The night certainly couldn't end worse than it began.

Marcie opened the door and stepped out into the oven-hot air. With her legs a bit unsteady, she took in the sight of Hook's home. The boxy, modern style wasn't one seen frequently in the desert, and was quite the step up from the trailer park all three of them grew up in. Managing the only garage in town apparently paid well, though she wasn't naïve enough to believe that was the MC's only source of income.

Typically, desert residences were one story; cooling a second floor in the scorching heat of summer became quite pricey. Hook, however, had two stories, and the entire roof of the home was covered in solar panels. Why every house in the desert didn't have solar panels was something that always baffled her. Must have something to do with the large upfront expense, though the savings over the long haul were entirely worth it.

The intoxicating smell of grilling meat tickled her nose and her stomach growled in approval. Hook and Striker were just feet away. That knowledge calmed some of her nerves and comforted her. She'd missed them throughout the years. The two had been such an integral part of her childhood. Friends, protectors, and in Striker's case, a surrogate brother. Her feelings for Hook had never been quite so benign.

A car door slammed and Marcie jumped, spinning just in time to see Tanner emerge from a second taxi.

"What the hell?" she muttered. Reacting on instinct, she started to march toward him, but then thought the better of it. He'd have to be completely stupid, besides being an asshole, to actually try anything out here with Hook and Striker just a scream away, but she'd be the stupid one to test the theory.

Tanner's footsteps crunched along the gravel.

"You need to call that driver back here right now. You aren't welcome here and you're not coming in with me. How the hell did you even know where to go?"

He smirked and her blood went from the normal ninety-eight degrees to boiling in an instant. "I remembered the address that your *friend* gave you."

Marcie took a calming breath and willed her legs to cease trembling. "I'm serious, Tanner. Hook and Striker aren't like your friends. You don't want to mess with them." The urge to punch that smug grin off his face was almost more than she could resist.

Fine, his funeral. "You know what? Knock yourself out, asshole. Just remember this conversation when one or both of them are kicking your ass."

As she marched up the walkway, she attempted to absorb the quiet peace of the fading evening. It would not be ruined because of Tanner.

The door swung open before they reached it and Hook stepped out, his eyes darkening with lust the moment they landed on her.

"Hey, Hook. I brought you some brownies from Sugar Rush bakery." She winced. Could she sound any more like a pissed off woman hoping to fool everyone with phony brightness?

Apparently not. Or at least she wasn't fooling Hook. He shifted his focus beyond her and his gaze iced over. "Hey, gorgeous. I see you still remember the way to my heart." Brownies had been Hook's all-time favorite treat when they were kids. If the beaming smile he threw her, despite the murderous look he tossed Tanner, was any indication, he approved of her offering.

He took the dessert and kissed her cheek. For a friendly hello, he lingered a bit too long. "What the fuck is he doing here?" he whispered against her ear.

A shiver raced down her spine at the feel of his lips barely brushing the sensitive skin of her ear. "He followed me. Apparently, he has a death wish," she whispered back.

"Hmm. No problem. The more the merrier." Hook returned to his full height.

Huh? What the hell? He was just going to let Tanner bust in on their evening?

"Tanner." Hook nodded at the other man, but his voice was frosty despite the warm evening.

A lump formed in Marcie's throat. No. He wasn't just going to invite Tanner in. He had something up his sleeve.

With a mischievous grin, Hook threaded his arm across her shoulders guiding her into his home. "I'll give you the tour later. Striker is manning the grill out back and I don't trust his ass with my beefy beauties."

Marcie laughed as they entered the house. Hook didn't give her much of a chance to scope the place out as he propelled her straight through to a set of sliding glass doors that led to the backyard. Stepping out, she gasped at the surprising beauty of his property. "Wow, Hook! This is amazing."

"Thanks, babe. I've had it for a few years. Did most of the rehab and landscaping work myself. It was a hole when I purchased it. The effort has kept me out of trouble…mostly." He winked and she laughed.

A large pavers-stone patio with an artistic pattern spanned much of the yard. On the left edge of the patio, an impressive grill station was set up. A huge stainless grill, mini-fridge and small work area were lined up and made from stone as well. In the middle of the patio, a round table that could seat eight sat surrounded by comfortable looking plush chairs. And on the far right, a stone fire pit rose from the patio with a double chaise lounge and three armchairs around it.

It was obvious Hook spent a lot of time out here and it was an impressive setup. The man surprised her. Never would she have guessed that the rebel she knew growing up would have such a domestic space.

"Hey there, beautiful." Striker gave her a quick and more appropriate peck than Hook had. "Pretty impressive, huh? Hook basically lives out here, it's his sanctuary."

"It's truly fantastic. You'd have to drag me back inside kicking and screaming if I lived here."

"Fanfuckingtastic," Tanner mumbled behind her.

Hook

With a sigh of frustration, Marcie ground her teeth together to keep the multitude of angry words inside her mouth. Losing her cool wasn't exactly the picture she wanted to present to Hook.

Besides, it took enough of her brainpower to ignore the fact that the instant she walked into Hook's house she had an overwhelming sense of being exactly where she belonged.

Hook had had just about enough of that dickhead. He hadn't so much as uttered a greeting since he'd been here and now he was trying to send Marcie some kind of subtle insult. Why the hell did he even bother to show up?

"Uhh, what's he—" Striker shut up when Hook shot him a death look. He wanted to see what the asshole's game was. Why he'd come. What he wanted from Marcie. Easiest way to do that was to let the shithead in for a bit.

"Well, anybody want a beer?" Striker asked.

"I can grab some if you trust me in your house. They in the fridge?" Marcie stepped backward, her thumb pointing toward the house over her shoulder.

Since it was apparent Marcie wanted a second to escape, Hook allowed her to go in and get the beer even though he had a few chilling in the mini-fridge next to the grill. "Yeah, babe, kitchen is to the right when you walk in."

The second she slid the door closed and was out of earshot both he and Striker turned their attention to Tanner. Hook spoke first. "Fuck's your problem, man?"

Tanner rounded on them. His eyes were glassy and he puffed out his chest like an overgrown peacock. "What's my problem? Hmm, maybe it's the fact that my girl and I are spending our vacation taking a trip down memory lane with two guys she spent her teenage years fucking."

Striker's face hardened with fury, while Hook looked on mildly amused. The thought of Striker touching Marcie with anything other than brotherly fondness was comical, as his friend had treated her like a beloved kid sister from the moment he met her. Hook, on the other hand, had one too many fantasies about fucking her in the past, and fully planned to fuck her in the very near future.

"She told you she fucked us?" Striker's voice reflected his shock.

"No fuckin' way she'd say something like that," Hook said. "Never even came close to happening. She was a fuckin' kid. And you're a piece of shit."

"You take turns with her? Or did you double team her? Her mother was a whore. Looks like the apple didn't fall too far." Tanner slurred and wobbled on his feet.

Great, a belligerent drunk. Just what Hook wanted to deal with.

"Is this guy for real?" Striker balled a fist and took a step forward, ever ready to step up for Marcie.

"Hold up, Striker." With a hand out, Hook warded his friend off. "Marcie is no doubt watching through the kitchen window right now. Her mother died this week and she's back here for the first time in ten years. She's got a lot of shit to deal with now. I don't want to upset her further." He focused his attention on Tanner. "And as far as I hear things, Marcie is no longer your girl. So, you get one more chance tonight, asshole. Sit down, eat your steak, and shut the fuck up. I'll kick the shit out of you myself if you blow it." Hook turned and strode toward his house, wanting a few moments alone with the woman who'd set up camp in his head and didn't seem to be leaving anytime soon.

He found her at the kitchen sink, watching out the window as predicted. Both hands rested on the edge of the sink and she was bent slightly forward, putting her in the perfect position for him to lift her dress over her ass and plunge into her from behind. His cock awakened at the thought, lending its approval, and his hands itched to palm the shapely globes.

Speaking of that dress... She wore a little yellow sun dress that cupped her pert breasts and allowed just a peek of cleavage. Two tiny straps held the entire thing up and Hook had visions of ripping them off and peeling the dress down her body. His favorite part, though, was how the fabric hugged her hips and ass as it fell halfway to her knees.

Marcie must have realized he'd come in the house since she watched the scene from the window, but she made no move to acknowledge his presence. No matter, going to her was no hardship.

He came up behind her and pressed his erection against her ass, wishing there was no clothing between them. Hook wrapped one arm around her lower abdomen and wound the other just below her breasts. He couldn't resist feeling the weight of them resting on his forearm.

"What the hell is this thing you're wearing?" he whispered against her ear, enjoying her shiver as his warm breath and lips caressed her skin.

Her back rumbled against his chest as a husky laugh slipped out. "You don't like my dress?"

"Are you kidding? This thing makes you look young and innocent, like a good girl who wouldn't be caught dead with some badass bikers. But we know differently, don't we?"

"Umm..."

Hook slid one hand up her torso to the bare skin above her neckline while the other hand splayed across her flat stomach, anchoring her against him. His wandering hand dipped down into the top of her dress, curling around a plump breast. "Jesus," he whispered when he encountered the braless flesh. "Definitely a little bit of naughty girl in there, huh, baby?"

"Hook..." She gasped and her head fell back onto his broad shoulder as his fingers found her nipple. He pinched it between his thumb and forefinger, drawing a tortured moan from her tempting lips.

"What, baby?" Taking advantage of her exposed neck, he added his lips to the sensual assault, kissing along the column of her throat.

"What are you doing to me?" She trembled and wiggled her ass against his groin.

A sharp gasp ripped from somewhere deep within him. "What I want to do, baby, is make you come. Then I want to fuck you hard, right here. So hard you can't even imagine going back to the motel."

"Yes, Hook, please." She sounded desperate and needy, just how he wanted her.

Unfortunately, they'd have to save any games until later because the two other men were waiting outside and were bound to come looking for them at any time. That was, if Striker could resist killing Tanner.

"It will have to wait, beautiful. Striker and Tanner are getting impatient."

At the mention of Tanner's name her shoulders sagged. "Why didn't you kick him out?"

"I don't trust him. I'm keeping my enemy close."

"We've only been together a few weeks. The relationship was nothing serious." She spun in the circle of his arms. "I don't date much. My boss set us up so I felt kinda pressured into it. Figured there wasn't any harm in having something to do a few nights a week." She shrugged as though it was enough of an explanation. "I was thinking of breaking it off when my mom died. He offered to come with me though, and the thought of having at least some support was too good to pass up."

Marcie had never trusted easily, her upbringing and her mother saw to that. For some reason, she'd placed all her young trust in him and Striker, but never let anyone else in. He wondered if she'd spent the ten years in Seattle much the same way. Alone. No family. Minimal connections. "You don't need to explain yourself to me. But I'd have been here for you in a heartbeat, baby. Striker, too."

She traced a finger over the letters of the words *No Prisoners* on his T-shirt, her gaze on the action instead of his face. "I closed that chapter when my mom moved us away. I was in college by the time she came back so I didn't come with her. We weren't speaking at that point anyway." She shrugged and finally lifted her gaze.

The sadness and loneliness reflected in her gaze squeezed his heart like a vice.

"That time in my life was so full of chaos. I was weak, ashamed. I don't like to remember who I was then. Plus, I had too many muddled feelings where you were concerned. So I never let myself think about you."

"Babe, you were a kid." There was so much more Hook wanted to say to her, starting with begging her to stay in Crystal Rock, but could he ask that of her? She had a job, a life in Seattle. How selfish would it be to ask her to stay? He almost laughed out loud. They'd been back in each other's lives for less than a full twenty-four hours. Of course, he couldn't ask her to stay.

"You sure he got the message that you broke up?" Responding to her confession of feelings would have to wait.

She huffed out an exasperated laugh and shook her head. A lock of golden hair fell across her forehead and Hook brushed it aside. "Apparently, he doesn't accept my breakup." She looked away again and as a cloud moved across her face.

That answer only aroused more questions. Hook gripped her chin between his thumb and forefinger and turned her face back to his. "Did the fucker lay a hand on you? Did he hurt you?"

"Not really."

"Not really?" Hook didn't want to scare her, or bully her, but he wouldn't accept a lie. And he wouldn't accept her covering for Tanner. "Babe." His voice was full of soft warning which he tempered by releasing her chin and stroking a finger along her soft cheek. "There is only one acceptable answer to both of those questions. And it's no, he did not touch me. No, he did not hurt me. Anything else is the same as a yes I need you to be straight with me right now."

She sighed and turned her head until her lips met his palm. She pressed a chaste kiss that should not have sent a shock of electricity straight to his dick. But it did. "He said some shit, scared me a bit, and was a little...rough. But no, he didn't actually hurt me."

Later, when he looked back on this, Hook would be really proud of the way he kept his cool despite the rage brewing in his gut. It was quite obvious Marcie downplayed Tanner's *rough* treatment. Well, fuck that.

Time to take out the trash.

CHAPTER EIGHT

Oh shit! "Hook! Hook, wait!" Marcie scurried after the very heated biker who stormed out of the kitchen intent on slaying her dragons.

Shit, shit, shit. She wanted Tanner gone as much as they did, probably more, but she didn't want anyone injured, or any damage to Hook's hard-won property. And she wanted to rid herself of the problem on her own.

She raced out the sliding doors and reached the patio just as Hook reached Tanner. He dragged Tanner up by the shirt, tromped across the patio and slammed Tanner's back against the stucco of the house.

Marcie winced. That must have hurt like hell.

"All right. Now we're talking." Striker turned from the grill, a huge smile on his face. "What'd he do now?"

"Hook! Don't do this." Marcie darted over until she was only a foot away from the men. Hook anchored Tanner to the house with a bulging forearm across her ex's chest. He shot Striker a searing look.

"On it, brother. Come here, baby doll." Striker jogged to her and wrapped a strong arm around her shoulders. He steered her farther away from the ensuing fight. Not that it would be much of a fight. Tanner didn't stand a chance in hell. Not if Hook's fighting skills were anything like what she remembered. Given that he was now named after a punch, she had a feeling his abilities had only improved. Growing up in in a seedy part of a rough town taught them early on how to defend themselves.

"Don't worry, hon. Hook's just gonna have a little chat with your man. I promise he won't kill him." Striker's laugh rang out above her head.

"He's not my man anymore," she muttered.

"Hook mentioned that. Guess Tanner wasn't too happy about that news."

"You could say that," she mumbled. This entire situation was so uncomfortable.

"Well then, I take it back." Striker's voice dropped to a lethal pitch. "Hook just might kill the fucker."

Annoyance scratched at the back of her neck. She wasn't a child. For the past eight years, she lived on her own, supported herself and didn't rely on anyone for anything. "Don't you guys think I'm old enough to take care of myself without my surrogate big brothers getting involved?"

Striker laughed again. "Baby girl, you may be *my* sister in all but blood, but you know damn well Hook would take you right here on this patio if Tanner and I weren't here. And no. When we're around, you'll never have to fend for yourself." He gave her an affectionate squeeze.

Marcie's face heated. Leave it to Striker to toss everyone's cards on the table. Despite the embarrassment, her heart warmed with a sense of family she hadn't experienced in ten years. Part of her wanted to protest. She didn't need any white knights to save her, but she couldn't deny the warm fuzzy feeling at knowing they cared for her.

"Fuck you, asshole. You think I'm scared of you or your club?" Tanner's belligerence sure wouldn't earn him any points with these two.

Hook spoke to a struggling Tanner, his voice too low for Marcie to make out, but the tone of the conversation was clear. Hook was pissed and Tanner was the reason. The longer Hook spoke, the more color drained from Tanner's face. She could only imagine the threats he issued.

Hook and Striker never knew, but she was well aware of the ass beating they'd issued the john that had accosted her when she was just ten. That was the start of them constantly looking out for her. It'd been one thing when she was a defenseless child with a grown man harassing her, but now, standing passively by and letting them handle her problems felt like taking the easy way out.

"Maybe I should say something." She glanced up at Striker who still wore a smile like he was very much enjoying the show.

"Nah, Hook's got this. He'll be done in a minute."

The urge to roll her eyes was hard to resist. She supposed they could just whip out their dicks and compare sizes. It would end this charade much faster. No doubt Hook's would be bigger.

Tanner nodded and finally stopped struggling against Hook's immovable hold. He glanced in her direction.

"Don't look at her." Hook's voice was loud and clear this time. "Striker will call you a cab. Your car will be done tomorrow morning and you'll leave town. Marcie isn't your concern anymore. Understand?"

Silence followed, probably only for five seconds but it might as well have been an eternity.

"Hey, buddy, you stupid enough to ignore the man's question?" Striker called.

Tanner looked at Hook and winced. Whatever he saw in the other man's eyes did the trick. "Understood."

Well, this afternoon certainly solidified her decision to buy a plane ticket home. Marcie held her breath as they waited for Tanner's answer. Silence stretched for long seconds. Could he really be stupid enough to defy Hook?

Tanner glanced at Marcie again. "She's a cold bitch anyway."

Striker grunted. "Fool," he muttered.

"I told you not to look at her. What makes you think I'm okay with you insulting her?" Hook's open palm cracked against Tanner's cheek and Marcie winced along with her ex.

Okay, enough was enough. "Hook! Just let him leave." She hardened her voice and tried to sound as stern as possible.

"Sorry, couldn't resist. Don't like how he keeps looking at you." Without releasing Tanner, Hook glanced her way, his eyes sparkling. "You sure I can't mess him up a little?"

This time she didn't bother to suppress the eye-roll. "I just want him to leave." She stepped forward, shrugging off Striker's arm and planted her hands on her hips. "Now."

Hook took two steps back, his forearm dropping to his side. Tanner sucked in strong gulps of air as though the pressure from Hook's hold had prevented his lungs from filling with oxygen.

"I'll be more than happy to escort our guest out and wait for his cab," Striker said as he stepped around Marcie and made his way to Tanner. "After you." With a flourish, he gestured toward the house.

Marcie didn't bother to watch Tanner scamper into the house. Her attention turned to Hook, who had returned to the grill. With a long pair of tongs, he removed the juicy steaks and potatoes from the heat. His posture was rigid, muscles bunched and tense, movements jerky. Only the rapid rise and fall of his back as he breathed let on that he was struggling to gather control.

Well that was just too damn bad. She had some things to say.

She let out a heavy sigh and walked with soft steps until she stood directly behind him. "Hook?"

"He won't bother you again, Marce." He remained focused on his task.

"Please turn around."

With a grunt, he closed the lid and faced her.

"Listen, Hook, I appreciate that you are willing to look out for me and help me, but I've been taking care of myself for quite some time. I don't need you to fight my battles for me."

His face darkened and his eyes narrowed to slits. "Oh really?" He waved a hand toward the door. "That was you taking care of things? Cuz it looked to me like the asshole put marks on your arm, then railroaded you and refused to leave you alone. But if I'm off base here, please feel free to correct me."

Oh, hell no, she'd just shed one jackass. No way was she going to acquire another. She stepped forward and jammed a finger into Hook's hard chest. Unfortunately, the feel of his muscles under the sensitive pad of her finger did more to distract her than get her point across. "Look, buddy, if I'm in over my head, I'll ask for help. I'm not stupid. All I'm saying is that I don't need you to play knight in shining armor. I'm not the same scared little girl I was when I left here. I'm actually fairly strong."

She let her hand drop. Touching him made her feel weak, needy. And in this moment, it was vital that he understand where she was coming from. Imperative that he understood her need for independence and self-reliance. She would not be the girl he knew ten years ago.

He grasped her face between his hands and lowered his mouth to hers. The brush of his lips was sweet, tender, but no less potent than the kisses he'd given her at the garage. She wanted to melt into him, forget all about standing on her own and let him take over. But she wouldn't, she couldn't. That girl had grown up and just didn't exist anymore.

Digging deep, she found the strength to break out of his embrace. Her mouth tingled and her mind spun, but she held her ground. "I need to know that you hear what I'm saying. That you'll let me handle my own life."

Oh gosh. That statement implied he'd have the chance to take over her life. That she planned to be a major player in his. What was she thinking phrasing it like that? She couldn't read him. His eyes swirled with powerful emotion, but she had no idea what it meant.

"Never once did I think you were weak, babe. Not then and not now." At least he ignored her other comment.

"Thanks," she whispered. But she knew the truth. She remembered the constant fear, the helplessness, and inability to care for herself as a kid. They'd just have to agree to disagree on that one.

"I hear Striker coming back. Let's eat. You must be starved." He retrieved the platter piled high with thick steaks.

Damn it looked good.

"I'm starved," she said. And she was. Starved for dinner, among other things.

CHAPTER NINE

Dinner was fun. Full of spirited conversation, laughs, and teasing. It was a strange feeling. Like old times yet also shiny and new. The three of them fell into a comfortable rhythm as though no time had passed, yet so much was different. Marcie was older for one thing—hell, all of them were—but it was most noticeable with her. Where she had been a girl the last time they'd all been together, she was a woman now. A gorgeous woman. A gorgeous woman Hook wanted in his bed more than he wanted his next breath.

Her bubbly personality emerged more and more throughout dinner. It was as though Tanner had been holding her back, stifling the real Marcie. Before he knew it, she was laughing and joking as if no time had passed. That sound, the joyful ring of her amusement, pulled all the blood to his cock and he spent the majority of dinner hard as a stone beneath the cover of the outdoor table.

"I feel like I've been rambling the entire time. You guys must be sick of hearing about me. Tell me everything that's happened around here since I left." Her eyes sparkled and her face had an adorable flush to it. Probably a combination of the heat of the day and the three beers she'd drank with dinner.

Hook didn't care how much she rambled on. He could listen to her all night. Listen to her and just watch her move in that provocative dress that made her look fresh and innocent. Christ, he was becoming a sappy motherfucker. Striker smirked at him like he knew the direction of Hook's thoughts. He flipped his brother the bird, discretely, so Marcie wouldn't notice.

"Actually, Marce, I gotta take off." Striker rose from the table, the shit-eating grin on his face even bigger than it as a second ago. The asshole would bust Hook's balls for weeks to come given the way Hook had been drooling over Marcie. "I have some shit to take care of at the clubhouse." He strolled around the table and dropped a chaste kiss on Marcie's head. She stared up at him with affection and love, but none of the smoky desire her green eyes held when she looked at Hook.

Thank God for that. And thank God Striker seemed to feel as brotherly toward her now as he had ten years ago. Because Hook would have one hell of a fight on his hands if Striker wanted more from her.

"Glad you're here, baby doll. I hope you'll think about sticking around for a bit."

Marcie stood and hugged Striker tight. "I just might do that." Hook met her gaze over Striker's shoulder. He'd do everything in his power to make sure she stayed. At least until they had the chance to explore the sizzling heat between them.

"Want to go for a ride with me?" he asked after Striker disappeared around the side of the house and Marcie returned to her seat.

She glanced at the setting sun then gave him a beaming smile. "I'd love to." She pointed to her dress. "But I'm not exactly dressed for it and it's already getting cool."

Damn, he couldn't wait to feel her wrapped around him on his bike. "I've got something to keep you warm."

She raised a sassy eyebrow and he barked out a loud laugh. "I mean a jacket, babe, but I like where your dirty mind is going." He winked and hopped up from the table. "Be right back." With quick steps, he darted into the house and retrieved the leather jacket he'd purchased for her earlier in the day. No question, he'd hoped this night would end speeding through the desert with Marcie on the back of his bike. Okay, so he hoped the night would end with screaming orgasms, but this was a perfect place to start.

"You just had that lying around, huh?" she asked as he emerged with the jacket.

Hook's face heated. Thank fuck Striker had gone. He'd torture Hook to death if he knew Hook was one step away from blushing. What the hell was it about Marcie that turned him into a fuckin' teddy bear? Well, that wasn't entirely true. He'd been more like a grizzly an hour ago with Tanner, and would be that way with any threat to her. Couldn't help it. He wanted to protect her, take care of her, wrap her in cotton and ensure nothing evil ever touched her. She'd known too much of that in her childhood. Didn't matter how much she professed she could take care of herself. He still wanted the job.

"I...uh...oh fuck it. I picked this up earlier today. Since I saw you last night, I've been dying to have you on my bike." Christ, was that just last night?

"Well, thank you." She reached for the offered jacket. "You're very sweet, Hook."

He grunted.

"Don't worry," she said as she slipped the jacket on. "I'll keep that to myself. Well? What do you think?" She twirled on her heel, arms out.

He swallowed. Maybe he'd just bend her over the table and fuck her right here. That flirty yellow sundress under the bad-girl leather jacket was enough to give him a stroke. "Smokin', baby," he said, adjusting his stance as the stiffness in his groin grew uncomfortable behind his jeans.

"What are we waiting for?" Marcie winked and sashayed past him, her hot-as-hell ass twitching just below the jacket.

Goddamn this woman fucked with his control.

Excitement zinged through Marcie's blood. She hadn't been on the back of a bike in...well, ten years. And then it had always been Striker's crappy old bike he'd worked his ass off to restore. She racked her brain trying to remember a time Hook had taken her on a ride on his junky bike, but couldn't recall any instances. Huh. Well she couldn't wait for it now.

She felt...good, light and happy. Tanner had been out of her life for just one hour and she already felt like a new woman. Although if she was being honest, Hook was primarily responsible for the giddy enthusiasm that practically had her bouncing after him toward his garage.

The heavy metal door slid up and Hook ducked under when it was about halfway open. Marcie followed suit and gazed around the garage. Two motorcycles—worlds nicer than what he'd had as a kid—and some kind of sporty-looking car filled the large space along with some tools, an extra refrigerator and a few cases of beer. Typical man stuff.

"Here, Marce."

She turned to find Hook standing next to one of the bikes, a shiny black helmet extended toward her. "Thanks," she said as she reached for the helmet. She worked it down over her short locks—which would look just fantastic after the helmet came back off—and fastened the clasp.

"Let me adjust it." Hook finagled the strap until it hugged her chin in a snug but not uncomfortable fit. "Good to go." He patted the top of the helmet and turned to the bike.

Marcie tried not to ogle his ass as he swung a leg over the bike and donned his own helmet. She really tried. But it was a useless effort. The man had a prime backside. What could she say?

"Hop on, babe."

"You know," she said as she slipped into position behind him and tried to tuck her dress under her legs, "I don't think I've ever been on a bike with you before. A million times with Striker, but never with you. Isn't that weird?"

Hook grunted. "No, babe. It's not weird. In about thirty seconds, you'll find out exactly why I never had you on the back of my bike." With that cryptic statement, he fired up the bike and rolled them out of the garage. "Ready?"

"You bet." Feeling like a kid on Christmas morning, Marcie molded herself to Hook's back and hugged tight around his waist. He twisted the throttle and shot off down the road.

And then, she got it. Fully understood the reason Hook hadn't allowed her teenage self to ride with him. All along her stomach and breasts, the corded muscles of his back bunched and flexed as he steered. His firm, bounce-a-quarter-off-it ass nestled in the V of her legs, providing just enough friction to make sitting still difficult. The position was perfection, like they were two puzzle pieces built to fit just so.

It was foreplay. Plain and simple. And her body reacted in the predictable way, dampening her panties and preparing her for something that might not happen. Could he tell? Could he feel the searing heat generated between their bodies? She should be ashamed, but the need rising inside her was fast overcoming any bashfulness.

Her nipples were hardened points that throbbed for his touch. Growing desperate for some kind of satisfaction, Marcie pushed her chest into his back. If she could just get the right angle. If the hard ridges of his muscles could just press into her nipples the right way, maybe she could find some relief from the deep ache.

Please don't let Hook notice. Christ, she was practically humping his back. He'd think she was a pervert for sure.

In the next instant, a strong hand landed just above her left knee. The heat from his palm seared her bare skin. And she thought she'd be cold without pants. She was going to spontaneously combust any second now.

Hook slid his hand up her thigh, giving a light squeeze before returning to her knee. He knew. That had to be his way of letting her know he was fully aware of her predicament.

Question was, what did he plan to do about it?

CHAPTER TEN

Hook was dying. Marcie was literally killing him one slow grind of her pussy against his ass a time. A whisper of a smile lifted his lips. She was in need, that was for damn sure. And who was he to deny her? Especially when his cock was mere seconds away from busting through his zipper?

He needed to find a spot to pull off the road. A spot that was private and secluded enough that he could bend her over the bike and fuck her like he'd been fantasizing. And he knew just where to go.

After cruising for another five minutes, Hook coasted to a stop on the side of the road. He and Striker used to bring Marcie to this very spot as kids. It was deep into the desert, a giant rock formation that arched over part of the road. During the day, the curving rock sheltered a small sliver of sand and road from the blistering sun. When life got shitty, as it often had, the three of them would escape out there and hide away from the heat of the day. Seemed a fitting place to bring Marcie tonight.

She climbed off the bike and removed her helmet, glancing around at her surroundings. If the smile on her face was any indication, she had fond memories of being here.

Hook couldn't take his eyes off her. She was gorgeous, a ray of sunshine and light. Short blonde hair framed her slender face in a way that was classy and spunky at the same time. Darkened by lust, her green eyes looked everywhere but at him. No doubt she felt some awkwardness for the way she'd rubbed all over him on the ride.

Hook was having none of that. She could use his body any time in any damn way she pleased and he'd take whatever she had to dish out with a smile on his face. Every single time.

"Marcie?" He swung his long leg over the bike and took a step toward her.

Finally, she met his gaze. The green of her irises was almost completely swallowed up by her dilated pupils. A red flush crept up her neck, settling in her cheeks. Embarrassment or yearning? Her pixie hair was mussed from the helmet, giving her a rumpled, bedhead look.

Hook could barely walk. His cock was so stiff, it filled his jeans to capacity. After three stilted steps, he reached her and grasped the edges of her open leather jacket. He could still feel the ghost of the hardened tips of her breasts stabbing into his back while she rode behind him. Now, he needed to see the evidence of her want.

He pushed the jacket over her shoulders, down her arms, and caught it before it fell. As he tossed it on the bike behind him, his gaze was riveted to the two points poking at her pale-yellow dress. "Christ, Marcie," he said. He couldn't touch her. Not yet. Not until he heard from her that she was on the same page. "Tell me you want this. Please tell me you want this as much as I do."

She shook her head and his stomach dipped to his knees. Had the buildup been all in his head? There was a chance he wouldn't survive the night if he couldn't find relief in her sweet body. She swallowed. "I think I might want this more than you do."

Hook huffed out a laugh. "Not possible, babe. Not fuckin' possible." He snagged her around the waist and pulled her flush against him. The hard ridge of his erection nestled into the welcoming softness of her stomach. Heaven. Pure fucking heaven.

He slid a hand up her neck, sifting his hand through the short strands of her hair. With a light tug, he tipped her head back until he had her mouth just where he wanted it.

"Don't make me wait," she whispered. "I've waited forever for you, Hook."

Wasn't that the fucking truth. Without a second of hesitation, he took her mouth in a fierce kiss. She opened for him immediately, curling her tongue around his and kissing him like she wanted him as much as he wanted her. The taste of her, the smell of her, the feel of her invaded all of his senses until everything in the universe that wasn't Marcie ceased to exist.

While they fought for control of the consuming kiss, Marcie curled one slender leg around the back of Hook's calf. She tightened her muscles and rocked her pelvis as though seeking friction to relieve an ache. He was too tall for them to line up properly in this position and she let out a low whimper when she couldn't find satisfaction.

Hook trailed biting kisses across her jaw, capturing her earlobe between his teeth. "You need me, baby?" he whispered after giving it a tug.

"Yes, Hook. So bad. You have no idea." She slipped her palms under his shirt and stroked the muscles of his back, her small hands igniting a fire of pleasure wherever they drifted.

"I've wanted under this damn dress all fucking afternoon." Hook skimmed his hands up the outsides of her silky thighs, under the dress until he encountered her panties. "Eyes on me," he said. With one hand, he pulled the soaked strip of fabric to the side, baring her folds for his touch. "Wet, baby, so fucking wet."

She moaned and bit down on her bottom lip as he sank his thick middle finger in her pussy. "Oh, God." She dropped her forehead to his chest. "Hook," she whispered.

He began a slow thrust in and out, taking care to press up and forward each time he sank in deep. Marcie's breathing sped up and whimpers of need flew from her mouth with every breath.

With her head buried against his chest, she gripped his biceps so hard he'd probably have welts later.

This was the most pleasure he could ever remember, and his cock was still fully covered and untouched. It went far beyond the physical sensations to a sense of complete rightness. Marcie was the woman he was supposed to kiss, supposed to pleasure, supposed to...love? Hell, he didn't know anything about love, but he knew he wanted Marcie. In his bed and in his life.

That should have freaked him out, would have if it was any other woman. But it was Marcie, and he was more than okay with it. Now, to figure out a way to get around her need to completely take care of herself and get her to let him in. Maybe even find a way to get her to stay.

Good didn't begin to describe the sensations Hook was wringing from her body. The encounter didn't compare to any of her past experiences. Because it was him. That had to be the reason.

He sank his finger in deep once again, this time swiping his thumb across her clit in the same moment. "Yes," she said, dropping her head back on her shoulders. Hook chuckled and brought his lips to her exposed neck.

"I need to see your tits." He spoke against her skin as he used his free hand to shove the straps of her dress down her shoulders. With a sharp tug, the front of her dress slipped down, baring her breasts to him.

"Christ," Hook whispered, his eyes riveted to her chest. "You're so damn pretty."

Her heart swelled at his words. Any response died in her throat when he cupped her breasts and ducked his head, sucking a nipple into the heated depths of his mouth.

"Ahh," she cried. Her hands flew to his head. He sucked with strong pulls while his finger still thrusted in and out and his thumb swiped circles around her clit. In seconds, she was moving her hips in time with his fingering as the world spun around her. "TJ," she whispered, not two minutes later. "I'm gonna come."

His given name leaving her mouth seemed to ramp him up even more and he groaned around her breast. "Let me feel it, baby. All over my hand. Now." He switched to her other breast, snagging the nipple between his teeth.

"Yesss," she yelled as the pleasure crested and all her muscles began a rhythmic clenching, including those of her pussy. It spasmed around his finger, trying to milk it as though it was his cock. She needed it to be his cock very soon.

Before she'd calmed, Hook was spinning her around and growling in her ear. "I need to fuck you. Right now."

"Please." She wanted to feel him filling her up. Wanted it more than she could recall ever wanting anything in her life. And she wanted him for so much more than these few stolen minutes. But she'd worked so hard to stand on her own. Hook would take over, guaranteed. He'd jump in, solve her problems, ease her path through life. A life she'd struggled to gain control of.

"You still with me, baby?"

She shook off the deep thoughts and came back to the moment. "Definitely with you," she said as her brain clued into the fact she was now bent over the bike with her dress bunched around her middle. Her breasts hung free, nipples brushing the cool leather of the motorcycle seat and her ass was on full display.

Hook slid his hands over the globes of her rear and gave a solid squeeze. It didn't matter where or how he touched her, every second of it was perfect. He hooked his talented fingers into the side of her bikini panties and drew them over her hips.

As he slid the material down her legs, he crouched behind her. "Step out." His face was level with her behind and his breath tickled the seam between her cheeks. Marcie lifted one leg and allowed him to work the panties over her foot. He stroked from the swell of her calf up to her inner thigh, coated with her juices and growing wetter by the second. "All for me, Marce. All for me."

"Yes," she said, lifting the other foot.

As she spoke, she looked over her shoulder and watched him dig a condom out of his back pocket. Then he lost his jeans and boxers, and rolled the latex down his impressive length.

Next time she'd be getting him in her mouth. It watered for a taste of all that alpha male strength. Her pussy clenched in anticipation as he positioned himself at her opening. "What are you waiting for?" The question was a desperate plea.

"Do you have any idea how fucking sexy you look right now? Bare to me, draped over my bike, waiting for my cock."

"Hoook." She moaned. "Please."

He chuckled behind her. "Yes, ma'am." He pushed into her, slowly, inch by inch until his balls met her skin and he was deeper than any man who'd come before him. Not that there had been many.

"Jesus, Marcie. Your pussy is tight. And hot as fuckin' flames." He drew out and rocked back in, beginning a steady rhythm.

"More, Hook. Give me more, harder." She wasn't above begging if she could get another of those brain-melting orgasms.

"Fuck, yeah," he whispered, his plunges becoming stronger, fierce. His hands were everywhere, her ass, her upper back, reaching around to pinch her nipples.

Marcie threw up a quick prayer in hopes that the force of his thrusts wouldn't tip the bike. She held the seat for dear life and met his hips with her own. The sound of heavy breathing, skin slapping skin, and the occasional harsh curse filled the now darkened evening air. She'd completely forgotten they were out in public, but no one ever came out this way. They'd never be discovered.

A tingling began low in her abdomen and spread out through her limbs. For a second, her wobbly legs threatened to fail her. But Hook, always in tune with her needs, snaked an arm under her hips and supported her. Maybe it wouldn't be so bad to give in to his support in some ways.

He tensed after two more thrusts, thrusts that hit a place inside her that created such an intense pleasure, her eyes literally crossed for a second. Before she expected it, she came so hard her knees buckled and she screamed his name into the wide-open desert.

The scenery blurred and she quaked in his embrace. Her fingers slipped from the motorcycle seat, no longer under her command. Hook was only seconds behind. He buried his face in her neck, shouting his release into her skin. His body jolted for long seconds before calming to nothing more than harsh breaths.

"Stay with me," he whispered against her ear.

She froze, just for a fraction of a second, but she feared he noticed. Should she stay? Could she stay? Would she depart too far from the independent woman she'd created over the past ten years?

"Just for a few days." He pressed a kiss to her neck, then rose to a stand.

Shivers racked her as his sweaty torso peeled away from her. Now that the frenzy was over, she realized the night had cooled considerably and she was quite cold.

Of course, he meant just a few days. They'd been back in each other's lives such a short time. She was crazy to think he meant for her to stay permanently.

He helped her stand, righted her dress, and assisted her back into the leather jacket. It was nice to have someone take care of her. More than nice. Maybe she'd gone so far overboard with her need for independence that she forgot what it was like to have someone care. Tanner certainly never did squat for her. Neither did her last few boyfriends. A chill settled over her that had absolutely nothing to do with the dropping temperature.

Was she picking assholes on purpose? Choosing men who didn't care enough about her to bother butting into her affairs so she could remain a liberated female? It was a sobering thought. One she'd have to give more time to later.

For now, she smiled up at Hook. "I'd love to stay with you for a few days."

At least.

CHAPTER ELEVEN

Morning sunlight streamed through the window, heating the room and counteracting the chill of the air conditioning. Hook kept his house at ice box temperatures. Not that Marcie minded much. He'd done a damn good job of keeping her warm through the night.

And what a night it had been. Hook was insatiable, and she'd found herself right there with him each time. Never had she experienced this passion with another man. This driving need to have him again and again. It was probably just the fact that she'd wanted him for as long as she could remember. The novelty would wear off. Wouldn't it?

Even now, with him curled around her back, his arm and leg trapping her to the mattress, she felt the stirrings of renewed desire. He shifted against her and let out a small snore. Marcie giggled, the motion jiggling her in his arms. Against her backside, a hard ridge began to form. Looked like the night of never ending pleasure wasn't quite over.

Buzz buzz.

Her phone vibrated on the unfinished surface of the nightstand. With a sigh, she snatched it up. Real life could have given them a few more hours before it barged back in.

You're crazy as well as a bitch if you think this is over.

Shit. Tanner.

Hook

He was supposed to pick up his car today and be on his way back to Seattle. There wasn't any reason for him to stick around and his friends had to be back anyway. He was probably just pissed at the way yesterday went down and this was his hissy fit. She didn't relish running into him when she returned home.

"Everything okay?" Hook's gravely morning voice rumbled in her ear.

She dropped the phone back on the night table and squeezed his hand that rested over her abdomen. "All good. Just someone from home." Not really a lie.

"Anything I can help with?" He nuzzled his nose in the crook of her neck and she shivered.

"No, Hook. Despite what you may think, I can actually take care of my own life." The bite in her own voice had her wincing.

"Whoa." He cupped her breast and thumbed her nipple.

The act had the intended effect and desire overtook her momentary snit.

"Baby, I'd never think otherwise."

"Sorry," she said as her back arched, pushing her breast farther into his hand and grinding her ass into his now full-blown erection. "Sore spot."

His hand felt so good, so strong and warm as it left her chest and stroked down her stomach, stopping right before he reached the place she needed him most. He stroked back up again and she understood why cats purred. It was hypnotic.

This time, when he reached the end of her body, he kept going. He teased her slippery folds with light touches. God, she wanted him inside her so bad she'd kill for it. Her eyelids fluttered closed as she anticipated the pleasure of his finger sinking into her.

"Tell me what it was like when you moved."

Her eyelids popped open. "What? Now?" Was he crazy? There was only one thing her brain could focus on, and it wasn't the story of her life.

"Yes, now. I used to know every damn thing about you and now you're practically a stranger. Tell me about your life." He bit down gently on her shoulder as his thumb glanced over her clit.

There was no way to hold in the moan. His touch was just enough to ignite a raging need, but not enough to extinguish the fire. "Jesus, Hook, you're killing me."

"Talk to me, babe. I'll make it worth your while."

"Okay, um, well you know we left because my mom met someone who was going to change our lives in miraculous ways." The bitter mockery was obvious even to her own ears.

"Not how it ended up?" He swirled the tip of his finger in her opening and her hips rocked forward. She needed that digit inside her.

"Shh, baby, you'll come...eventually. I promise. Just tell me your story."

She growled and he chuckled as he resumed the feather-light touches and torturous strokes to her folds. "Actually, things were pretty good for a while, but you know what they say. A leopard doesn't change its spots. About a year after we moved, my mom's boyfriend discovered she'd hooked up with a pimp at some point and was whoring herself once again." She shook her head, lost in the story now. Hook's hand moved from between her legs and smoothed up and down her back in a soothing motion. Now that she'd started, the words tumbled out.

"I have no idea why she did it. She didn't need to. For the first time in our lives, she had money, she had security, she had a man that actually gave a shit about her. It was like an addiction for her, a habit she couldn't kick."

"I'm sorry, Marce. She wasn't nearly as strong as you are. Some people don't feel they deserve happiness."

She shrugged. "I'm sure you're right and I should be a bit more sympathetic. It's just hard for me to do that." It was nearly eight years ago now, shouldn't bother her anymore. "Anyway. Her boyfriend kicked us out. I found out what she'd been up to at the same time he did, but he lumped me in with her and

Hook

refused to talk to either of us. We moved to a shitty apartment and she used to fuck men for money more often than not. At the time, I had about six months of my senior year in high school left. I worked my ass off. Got two after school jobs. I wanted out. With the help of financial aid and an academic scholarship I was able to go to a local college and live on campus. We only spoke a handful of times after I moved out.

"I did well in college, worked multiple jobs the entire time, graduated, and started my career. I didn't need her. Everything I've accomplished since we moved away has been one hundred percent on my own, with hard work and grit. I'm happiest when left to take care of myself."

The statement didn't hold quite the punch it was supposed to. It was hard to assert her independence when she lay in Hook's arms, seconds away from begging him to fuck her.

Anger sizzled just below the surface of Hook's calm façade. There was a big difference between being independent and being abandoned her whole life, and Marcie didn't seem to recognize the distinction. She wasn't meant to be alone and lonely. The way she responded to him last night and now was a testament to the way things should be. She was meant to pleasure and be pleasured. To be part of a team. To be loved.

But how to convince her of this? Her heart was akin to an abused animal who didn't trust its new owner. He would just have to show her how much better life could be if she shared her burdens and workload with someone.

"I'm proud of you, baby. You took a shit situation and came out shining." The softest skin he'd ever felt glided under his fingers. Not touching her wasn't possible.

"Thank you," she whispered, her voice full of emotion. She believed him. Good. Her body was strung tight as a violin string and she moaned as he slipped his hand between her legs once again, pressing his palm against her mound. Playing with her was more fun that he'd had in years. She'd go off like a fucking firecracker when he finally let her come. If anyone needed a release right now, it was her.

"Hook, please." She ground her pelvis into the heel of his hand, no doubt trying to rub her little clit against him and get herself off. Greedy. He loved it.

"You're so hot here, Marce. Tell me what you need." He licked up a corded tendon in her neck and she whimpered.

"I need to come, Hook. I need to come so bad. You're killing me." She trembled in his arms, on the verge of a powerful release.

Without another word, he shoved two fingers up into her channel and curved them forward with an almost rough stroke. She detonated at once, like a live bomb whose timer had just run down.

"Hook, Hook," she cried. "Shit, oh my God."

It seemed to go on forever. Damn, he wished he could see her face, but as he was still spooned around her back, he had to content himself with her cries and shudders of pleasure. When she calmed to the occasional small tremor, Hook withdrew his hand from her pussy and rolled her to her back. Satisfied eyes, glazed with pleasure, met his gaze. "You okay, baby?"

"I—" She swallowed. "Hook, I've never...I mean that was... intense." Her expression held a hint of shyness.

It was intense. The entire night had been intense. Different. They connected on a level that went far beyond the physical. He had no idea what the hell to do about it. The only thing he was certain of in this moment is that the wanted more of Marcie. Beyond that...well, he was clueless.

Lying beneath him, her eyes were soft and dewy, her cheeks flushed from the recent orgasm, and her hair stood on end in an adorable chaotic pattern. He traced her lower lip with the pad of his finger, coated with the evidence of her arousal. Almost as if by reflex, her tongue darted out and followed the trail of his fingertip. As her own flavor tickled her senses, the green of her irises disappeared around the edges of her widening pupils.

He needed a taste for himself. His lips met hers and her spicy essence filled his senses. Lost in her intoxicating flavor, Hook didn't register her movements until she'd flipped their positions and sat between his thighs, a mischievous gleam in her gorgeous emerald eyes.

With a wink, she shimmied down the bed until she was eye level with his very hard cock.

His throat thickened and he swallowed as best he could around the lump of anticipation. This was his number one fantasy, right here. Marcie between his legs prepared to take him in her mouth. If she had any idea the number of conscious and asleep fantasies he'd had about this very thing over the years, she just might think he needed some professional help.

With her gaze trained on his—there was no way in hell he'd miss this visual—she gave him a long, slow lick from root to tip.

"Holy fuck." His hips jerked and his shaft bumped her mouth, like it was trying to find its way between her lips. After a sly smile, her tongue came out again, this time circling the sensitive head. "Suck me, baby, take me deep."

"So, Hook, tell me what you've been up to the last ten years. I used to know everything about you, and now you're practically a stranger." She spoke against the tip of his dick and his eyes rolled back in his head.

"Shit." His head dropped back and he stared at the ceiling. The pixie would be the death of him. But what a way to go. Death by sexual torture.

She chuckled, the sound a combination of desire and the knowledge that in this moment she held one hundred percent of the power. There wasn't a damn thing he wouldn't give to her for the pleasure of having her suck his cock.

"Well, the club gets most of my time and attention. I prospected with Striker shortly after you left."

"Does your family still live here?"

"Nah, they moved back to Australia about five years ago."

"You in touch with them?"

He lifted his head and shot her a look. "Seriously? My childhood may not have been quite what yours was, but there's no love lost between us. You know how it was. They moved us to the US with dreams of Hollywood stardom and ended up little more than junkies who had the unfortunate luck of being saddled with a kid." He shrugged. This was such old news, but he supposed they never had talked about it as kids.

"I'm so sorry, Hook. It's their loss. And now you work at the garage?"

He appreciated how she didn't harp on the difficult part of his younger years. "Yeah. Actually, I manage it. Shiv, he's the club's president, promoted me, oh, about two years ago now."

"Well, it sounds like you've carved out a nice little life for yourself." There was genuine admiration and affection in her voice.

"Can't complain, babe. Well, there's one thing I could complain about right now." He narrowed his eyes and tried to spear her with a severe look, but she giggled and looked so fuckin' hot hovering over his dick that he couldn't help but grin at her like a lovesick fool.

"I suppose you gave me what I wanted." She lowered her head and sucked him into the wet heat of her mouth, taking him all the way to the back of her throat. Her hands massaged his thighs and her throat muscles worked the head of his cock as she swallowed around him.

"Christ, Marce, that mouth." Stars floated in his darkening vision and his head dropped back on the pillow once again, pleasure overtaking his ability to command his muscles. He closed his eyes and let the overwhelming sensations take over as Marcie proceeded to blow his mind.

One thing was for sure, a man could get very used to this kind of treatment.

CHAPTER TWELVE

It had been three days of living with Hook.

Three days of consuming, physical pleasure that seemed to get better each time.

Three days of an emotional connection that rocked her to her core.

Three days of harassing text messages from Tanner.

At first, the name calling and thinly veiled threats pissed her off. Then he sent a photo of himself sitting on her couch with the words, *Can't wait until you come home,* and she was now officially freaked out.

Tanner was obviously stupid as well as crazy, if he thought she'd just roll over and take this nonsense. She'd been able to file a police report by phone and the officer who responded assisted in coordinating a locksmith to change the locks and add a few extra deadbolts. She'd look into a security system of some kind when she returned, which would have to be sooner rather than later.

The police wanted to speak with her in person, though they understood she'd be out of town for a few more days. They needed her to assess her apartment and make sure nothing was stolen or vandalized. The police wanted access to her phone as well and instructed her not to engage with Tanner, but to keep the text messages and voicemails so they had an accurate record of each and every contact.

Buzz buzz.

Oh geez, not again. She glanced around the No Prisoners clubhouse, at the four men who chatted and seemed oblivious to her presence. They'd invited her to a meeting so she could help plan a big party for Striker. The club was about to vote him in as vice president.

Should she check the text now? No one was paying attention to her, and it would drive her nuts if she didn't read the message. As slyly as possible, she lifted her phone and snuck a peek at the screen.

Miss you, baby.

What? Seriously? It was time to consider the fact that there was a high possibility Tanner had a very real psychological disorder. As instructed, she ignored it, but kept the message on her phone.

"Marce? You okay, babe?" The obvious concern in Hook's voice cut through her musings.

Apparently, she sucked at keeping a neutral expression, which was why she'd hesitated to check the phone in the first place. Hiding Tanner's frequent contact and her multiple conversations with the Seattle police department from Hook had been no easy feat. But it was necessary. If he found out, he'd leave a trail of dust and gravel as he shot off toward Seattle to take care of Tanner himself. She was handling it just fine on her own.

She dropped the phone back to the table with a clatter and swallowed. Four very large, very tattooed, very hard bikers stared at her. Whoops. How much of the conversation had she missed? "Ah, sorry, guys, zoned out for a second. Can you repeat the last thing you said?" Hopefully she hadn't missed more than a statement or two.

The biggest of the bunch, who sat directly across from her at the rectangular tables chuckled. "Sure, doll," he said. What had Hook said his name was? Jester, maybe? "I just asked if you'd ordered the food for the party."

"Yes, I did. Let's see." She flipped through the pages of her notebook. "I ordered enough food to feed an army." She cast a sideways glance at Hook, only to see he still looked at her with undisguised concern.

"Great," Jester said. The man really was huge. He stretched his arms over his head and nearly took out the lanky man next to him with his crazy wingspan.

Gumby, his name was, the tow truck driver from a few days ago.

"What about you? You good for booze?" Jester asked Gumby.

"Yeah, everything will be delivered to Hook's tomorrow evening around five, which I realize is right during the vote."

"No worries," Marcie said, relieved to be on the ball this time. "I'll be at Hook's all day setting up for the party. Does Striker know about it?"

From the head of the table, Shiv laughed. He was a fierce character, a bit older than the others with a dark, close-cropped beard and hair that hung well past his shoulders. A jagged scar ran down his left cheek giving him an intimidating appearance. "He knows about the VP vote, but not the party."

"So what happens if he doesn't get voted in as vice president?" Apparently, it was a stupid question if the laughter that rose around the table was any indication.

"No way that will happen, baby. Striker's a shoe-in for VP," Hook said.

"All right," Shiv pushed from the table and stood. "Sounds like everything is under control. Party at Hook's tomorrow, starts right after the vote and goes until no man, or woman, is left standing."

Snickers went around the table and Marcie raised a brow at Hook. He winked and turned away to answer something Jester had asked him. From what she'd heard her entire life, No Prisoners' parties were legendary. Under normal circumstances they were held at the clubhouse, but everyone figured Striker would be expecting that and they could have a little fun at his expense by switching up the location. Hopefully she could keep up with these wild bikers. Not to mention the interesting gaggle of ladies that were expected to make an appearance.

Growing up, her mom had been to a number of parties at the clubhouse, and she recalled a few instances where she'd *entertained* club members in their trailer. It was a bit disconcerting to be an adult now attending one of these parties, especially knowing there would be women there like her mom. Women looking for one thing and one thing only.

"You ready to go, hon?" Hook whispered in her ear.

"Yes, can we stop for something to eat on the way home? I'm starving."

He gave her a quick fierce kiss that fired her blood in an instant. "Grab your bag. I'll just say bye to the guys and we'll stop at that pizza place you used to love."

With a smile, she ignored the pitter patter of her heart. He remembered so many things she enjoyed from their teenage years. How was a girl supposed to resist such a sweet man? "That place is still there?"

He rose from the table. "Sure is, babe. And still the best pie around."

She stood by as he hugged and back-slapped his buddies. Even if she hadn't known how the MC operated, how loyalty to the club and their brothers came above all else, it was obvious how close these men were. They teased each other mercilessly, but underneath it all was a core of respect and love.

She had none of that in her life. No one who cared for her in such a deep way. No one was loyal to her with that strength. And now that her mother had passed, no family to speak of. Not that her mom had been anything in the way of family. Was it any wonder she fought so hard to be self-reliant?

What choice did she have when she was the only one around?

"Hey, babe? I'm going to move some wood from the garage to the back of the house so we'll have it for the fire pit tomorrow,"

Hook said when they entered his kitchen an hour and a half later.

"Want help?"

"Nah, go take a shower like you said you wanted." He grabbed her hips and tugged her close, rocking her against his semi-erection. "If you're still in there by the time I'm done maybe I'll join you."

With a sassy wink, she looped her hands around his neck. "Guess I'll be taking a long shower then."

He kissed her quick then spun her around. "Get movin' before I jump you right here."

"That's not what you say if you want me to leave," she called over her shoulder.

"Go, babe." He gave her a quick slap on the ass and laughed when she yelped and took off for the stairs.

He lingered a minute, watching the back and forth sway of her rounded ass as she ascended the steps. At some point, they needed to have a conversation about what was happening between them. For the past three days, they'd lived in domestic bliss, something Hook never thought he'd enjoy, but there was no point in denying it. He fucking loved every second of her living in his house and wanted it to continue, for the rest of his life if he had any say.

He was just too chicken shit to bring it up because her feelings weren't obvious. Tomorrow. After the vote, after the party, they'd have a heart-to-heart. And he'd do his damnedest to convince her to stay.

Buzz buzz.

Marcie's phone vibrated against the kitchen table. He flicked a glance at the staircase, but she'd disappeared after reaching the top step. No matter, he could just run it up to her if it was anything important. After if buzzed again, he lifted it from the table and checked the message.

I've been nice for three days and you called the cops? Some punishment may be in order when you return home.

What. The. Fuck.

Hook scrolled through the messages. Forty-seven. There were forty-seven texts and fifteen voicemails from Tanner over the past three days. Some were oddly and sickeningly sweet while others held not so vague threats like the one that just came through.

She hadn't said a word. Not one fucking peep. This dickhead had been harassing her for days and she hadn't uttered a word. How many times had Hook fucked her silly over the past few days? Yet she remained silent. How many hours of conversation had they had about their lives? Lips still sealed. Well that was some right bullshit and not something Hook would tolerate.

He stormed up the stairs and slammed into the bathroom. Marcie stood under the spray, clearly visible through the glass shower door, her hands running through her short locks. She turned when the bathroom door bounced off the wall and a seductive smile graced her lips. "That was fast."

As mad as he was at her, the sight of soap bubbles sliding their way over her slick skin and over her curves caused him to react predictably. Blood rushed to his cock and it rose to attention. Damn thing knew exactly what it'd be missing out on due to the impending fight. Couldn't be helped. There were some things Hook would not abide by and threats to Marcie's safety were one of them.

With a low growl, he yanked open the shower door and held the phone out, ignoring the fact that water droplets splattered the screen. "What the fuck is this?"

Marcie's hands dropped to her sides and her face lost all color. "What are you doing with my phone?"

"It buzzed on the table and I thought I'd see if it was important. Turns out, it's really fucking important. How could you not tell me he's been harassing you? For days, Marcie! Days! Did you think I wouldn't be able to put a stop to it?"

"What?" Her nostrils flared and she jammed her hands on her hips. "I didn't say anything because I knew exactly what would happen. This! You'd get on your macho horse and feel like you have to take over and solve the problem for me. Well, buddy—" she jammed her soggy finger into his chest. "I don't need you or anyone to fix my shit for me. I'm taking care of it myself."

Hook raised his gaze to the ceiling and counted to ten. Or at least he tried to make it to ten. At around six, he nearly exploded. "You're goddamned right I'd put a stop to that shit. He's fuckin' threatening you, Marcie! I'm not trying to take over your life, babe, but there are some things a man cannot overlook when it comes to his woman. And another man threatening her is at the top of the list."

That was the first time he'd laid any verbal claim to her, and it wasn't lost on her. Her eyes filled with tears and she took a step back, farther under the spray. Shit. That couldn't a good sign.

"Look, this has been fun. Amazing, really. But we're just pretending. I don't live here. My life, my job, my apartment, they're all in Seattle. And I can't be with a man who doesn't allow me to handle my life my way. I called the police. They are dealing with Tanner. In fact, I need to get back to Seattle to meet with them. I think...um...I think I'll book a flight out for tomorrow."

It wasn't possible for her to look more vulnerable that she did in that moment, tears streaming down her face, arms crossed over her chest, naked. All he wanted was to gather her up and make them both forget the past ten minutes. But the problems would be waiting for them when the heat cooled.

"I'm not your mother, Marce. I won't abandon you. I won't make you promises I'm unwilling to keep. Yes, I want to take care of you. Yes, I want to help you with your problems. Yes, I want to be involved in every aspect of your life. But I want the same from you. For you to take care of me, be involved in every part of my life and help me with my problems. I'm not looking for a takeover. I'm looking for a partner and a lover. And that's what you're really afraid of. But go ahead and keep hiding behind this need for independence, because it seems to be working real well for you."

Was this what a broken heart felt like? This hollow emptiness in his chest? This feeling that everything good in his life was spiraling away faster than the water disappearing down the drain? If it was, he fully understood why he'd never offered his heart to a woman before. This shit hurt. "Don't go, Marcie."

She sniffed. "I have to."

"At least wait until after the party. You worked hard to help us put it together. You deserve to see it through." As much as he wanted to, he wouldn't force her to stay. But there was no way in hell he'd let her walk out that door without ensuring that Tanner wouldn't be a problem for her in Seattle. And for that he needed a little time.

With a sad smile, she shrugged.

Only one card in his deck had any chance of producing a winning hand. "Striker would be crushed if you weren't here to celebrate with him."

Furious emerald eyes met his gaze. "Fine. You win. I'll stay for the party. But I'm leaving when it's over. And I'm sleeping in the guest room tonight."

With her head held high she turned off the water, ducked under his arm, grabbed a towel, and slipped out of the bathroom. The sound of the guest room door slamming shut mimicked the closing coffin of their relationship.

Now what?

Now, he had about twenty-four hours to change her mind. And if that didn't work, he had twenty-four hours to ensure Tanner wasn't around to cause trouble for her in Seattle.

CHAPTER THIRTEEN

The party was a resounding success. All around her, men and women celebrated Striker's election to vice president. They ate, drank, danced, flirted, and did a few other eye-popping yet arousing things that were typically reserved for private locations. Instead of joining in the merriment, Marcie hung to the side and watched the crowd while her thoughts swirled like a violent cyclone.

Was Hook right? Did she hide a fear of abandonment behind the guise of wanting to be independent? A large part of her worried he was dead on. It made sense. She picked guys like Tanner, who wouldn't so much as slap a band-aid on her if she were gushing blood, forcing herself to manage everything on her own. Then, when the relationship inevitably failed, it didn't matter, because she didn't need them. These men didn't play any significant role in her day-to-day, so she was no worse off when they vanished.

What the hell was she supposed to do if she gave in to Hook? If she allowed him to help her, to be her partner? How would she endure if he one day changed his mind and no longer wanted her? Today, she was strong, independent, and capable of taking care of herself. Yes, walking away from Hook was going to gut her, but she would survive as she had in the past.

If she stayed? If she allowed him to solve her Tanner problem and do things for her, she'd inevitably lose that part of herself that was strong and self-reliant. Then what would happen when he was gone? She'd no longer be the woman she was today. No longer be able to dust herself off and move on. She'd have to start from scratch, learning to be independent and take care of herself all over again. There was a chance she wouldn't have the strength to build herself back up again.

Wasn't it just better to avoid the possibility of heartbreak altogether? A couple came into her field of view as she leaned against the side of the house and tried to blend into the scenery. She had no idea who they were, the man wasn't wearing a No Prisoners cut, but that was beside the point. They sat near the fire, whispering back and forth, stealing the occasional passionate kiss and making googly eyes at each other. They looked smitten, hopelessly in love.

And where was she? Guarding her heart like a junkyard dog, alone, and on the outskirts. She told Hook she'd be leaving after the party, yet she'd made no move toward any sort of plan to return to Seattle. Hadn't booked a flight. Hadn't rented a car. Hadn't packed so much as a sock in her suitcase. Her head was such a mess.

The couple locked lips again and Marcie had to look away. Her heart ached too much to witness other's blissful adoration.

"Okay, darlin', I have no idea what happened between you and Hook, but I'm done letting you throw your own pity party over here." Striker leaned against the wall next to her and held out an uncapped beer.

"Thanks. And congratulations."

"Thanks, hon." He pointed across the yard. "Hook looks even more wrecked than you do. You want to talk about it?"

Hook did look bad. Or sad, really. Standing in a group of laughing bikers, he wasn't engaged in the conversation, but scanning the crowd. Probably looking for her. In true cowardly fashion, she'd avoided him like the plague since last night. "No. No, I don't."

With a heavy sigh, Striker faced her. "I'm just going to say one thing, then I'll leave you alone. You're it for that man." He pointed toward Hook with his beer bottle. "Always have been. He stayed away years ago because you were way too fuckin' young and it would have been wrong. But it's not wrong now, and he wants you even more. He won't hurt you, Marce. Not like you're afraid of. That man will not abandon you. Ever." He pressed a kiss to her cheek then pushed off the wall. "Think about it," he called over his shoulder.

An ache formed between her eyes and she rubbed it. Was everyone onto her issues? She took a long drink from the frosty beer and when she lowered the bottle, her eyes locked with Hook's. He looked like every woman's fantasy with a T-shirt stretched across his powerful chest and jeans that hugged him in all the right places. But it was his gaze that held her captive. Sad and hopeful all at the same time.

Someone came and whispered in his ear. He nodded then shot her a wink mouthing *don't move*. It was time to face the music. Time to put on her big girl panties and talk to him. Time to admit that maybe she did have some hang-ups.

Damn, Marcie looked good in those tiny denim shorts with the form fitting yellow V-neck T-shirt. Yellow was such a great color on her. Sunny like her personality. She was so close to him, yet might as well be a million miles away for the emotional distance between them.

"You hear me, Hook?" one of the prospects asked.

"Yeah, man, sorry. You said the coolers need more beer?"

"Uh huh. Want me to fill them?"

"Nah, Prospect. I'll get it." The fewer people inside his house the higher the chance it wouldn't be destroyed by the end of the party.

He held up two fingers and mouthed *two minutes* to Marcie. Hopefully she'd wait for him. It'd been almost twenty-four hours since their fight and she hadn't spoken a word to him. In fact, she'd avoided him the entire day. Since she seemed to need a bit of distance, he gave her space to set up for the party and made himself scarce.

That had given him exactly zero opportunities to apologize properly and beg her to stay. Because he would beg if he had to. He just couldn't lose her. Not to mention the friends he contacted in Seattle to give Tanner a little talking to couldn't track him down. Neither could the police. He appeared to have vanished. Something was up there. Something that had his gut churning. Marcie needed to know, to be vigilant.

He stepped into the sizable room he used as an office on the first level of his house. Often times, after far too many hours at the garage, he brought paperwork home to complete in peace and quiet. The office served as a dedicated work space. Tonight, it served as extra beer and liquor storage. The temperature outside had soared during the afternoon, making it too hot to store the plethora of booze in the garage.

As he bent to retrieve a case of beer, something—or rather someone, based on the shape and feel of a male body—slammed into him from behind. Hook was an excellent fighter, but a sneak attack, an ambush from behind was nearly impossible to anticipate or defend against.

"What the—" The force of the assault caused a forward momentum Hook was helpless to avoid, and he crashed headfirst into the tall stacks of liquor-filled boxes.

Sounds of smashing glass filled the room as a tower of boxes came tumbling to the ground. Hook landed in the heap and grunted in pain as a final box plummeted into his shoulder. Shit. That was going to leave a significant mark. Not to mention the one that would be left by the sharp points of multiple boxes digging into his back.

One benefit to being a skilled MMA fighter was the ability to react instantaneously and be light on his feet, despite pain. Hell, pain was a given when a man's fists connected with his body, no matter how fit he was. Hook shook off the discomfort and flew to his feet, assumed a fighting stance, and prepared to demolish his enemy.

A quick scan of the room revealed he was alone. No attacker. No threat.

"What the fuck is going on?" he muttered.

The room reeked of alcohol thanks to the destroyed bottles and soaked boxes, but Hook ignored the mess. It would keep. Priority number one was assessing the threat level to his guests, and Marcie. Especially Marcie.

With a roll of his sore shoulder, Hook stepped over the downed boxes and stomped toward closed the door. The knob twisted easily, but when he pulled to open the door, it didn't budge. "Shit." With more force, he jiggled the knob yanked like his life depended on it. Which it looked like it did.

Nothing.

"All right. Very funny, fuckstick. Who the fuck is holding the fuckin' door closed? Stop hiding and confront me."

Crickets.

What the fuck was going on?

The shatter of glass spun him toward the window behind his desk. Dark gray smoke filled the room, singing his lungs and burning his eyes. "Fuck!" Orange flames licked up the long curtains and the wooden blinds ignited in a flash of heat.

He hurtled himself against the door again, to no avail. As he breathed in, his lungs spasmed, protesting the smoky poison that took the place of clean oxygen. Harsh coughs racked him and he dropped to his knees as the need for fresh air became imperative.

Christ, he had to get the fuck out of here. Something was seriously wrong; his house was under attack from an unknown enemy. Thoughts of Marcie flashed through his mind. Was she safe? Was she protected? Striker would move heaven and earth to keep her out of harm's way, but was he in any position to do so?

Hook squinted. Tears poured down his face as his eyes rejected the toxic burn of the smoke. He couldn't see two inches in front of his face, and his lungs screamed with the need for oxygen. If he could get behind the desk, he could throw himself through window and outside to where air, and possibly an ambush awaited. It wasn't an ideal solution as the entire window was engulfed in scorching flames.

Drop down. Wasn't that what he'd heard to do in a house fire? It couldn't make the situation worse. On shaking hands and knees, he crawled along the floor feeling for the desk.

With each fraction of an inch forward, the temperature grew more unbearable, until he could barely force his arms and legs to advance. Hook's arm flew across his face in a feeble attempt to block the searing heat. Dizziness swamped him and he jolted with fierce hacking coughs as he tried to suck in air. Darkness clouded his vision and memories of Marcie played through his mind.

He was going to die. The possibility of death was something all MC members faced at some point, and most didn't fear it, especially if it was in defense of the club. But dying with tension between him and Marcie? Dying without telling her he fucking loved her and wanted her in his life forever? That shit didn't sit well.

With a burst of energy, he drew his shirt over his mouth and nose and tried to crawl forward, but the need for oxygen won out and he collapsed in a prone position.

He kept Marcie at the forefront of his mind while darkness rimmed his vision. Marcie's face, Marcie's laugh, the way her pussy gripped him tighter and hotter than he'd ever experienced. The way she burrowed into his heart and made him love her with every fiber of his being.

Seconds before the blackness overtook him, Hook remembered the broken cases of spilled beer and booze.

Fuck.

The entire room was going to blow in a matter of minutes.

CHAPTER FOURTEEN

Pop pop.

Marcie may not have had much, if any experience with firearms, but she knew the sound of gunfire when she heard it. You didn't grow up in a horrible part of town with a parent who spent most of her time sleeping with men on the wrong side of the law without ever hearing the pop of a gun.

"Marcie, get the fuck down." Striker sprinted back toward her, his mouth in a grim line and a look of rage in his ice blue eyes.

His words kicked her into gear. She immediately dropped to the stone ground and crawled toward the edge of the house. Striker reached her by that point and jerked her around the house by the waistband of her denim shorts.

His inhalations were harsh and choppy, but his hands held steady as he peered around the corner, weapon at the ready.

Still on her hands and knees, Marcie drew in a breath and shook her head, trying to slow the rush of blood in her hears. She gripped Striker's leg and peeked around him into Hook's yard.

Tanner stood in the center of the yard, a wicked looking assault rifle in one hand and some poor trembling mess of a girl held tight against his body with the other. God, where had he gotten his hands on a weapon like that?

"No one gets hurt as long as Marcie comes out here in the next ten seconds." Tanner's hair was a mess, his clothes were rumpled, and a crazed look of the insane gleamed in his eyes. He'd completely lost his shit.

"Oh my God, Striker," Marcie whispered. "I need to go out there."

"Don't you dare move one muscle, babe. You take one step toward Tanner and I guarantee Hook will make it so you can't sit for a week. Just before he rips off my balls."

"Striker, he's going to hurt her." Her voice shook and panic worked its way up her throat. No way could she hide like a coward when someone's life was at stake.

"Look around, hon. There are armed bikers all over. He won't kill her, he'd be dead two seconds later. He needs her to get out of this alive. Your boy may be crazy, but he obviously didn't think this through too well."

The acrid smell of smoke irritated Marcie's senses. "Do you smell that?" She scanned the yard and looked down the length of the back of Hook's house. Black smoke poured into the air from the opposite side of the house.

"Oh my God, Hook. Striker, the house is on fire and Hook's in there." She tugged at Striker's jeans and pointed. Fear like she'd never known threatened to overtake her ability to function. Hook was in serious trouble; she knew it in her gut with one hundred percent certainty. "I have to get in there to help him."

With her pulse pounding hard, lightheadedness swamped her and she started to crawl back around the house. Only fifteen feet separated her from the sliding doors to Hook's house. If she went fast enough, there was a chance she could reach the door unseen by Tanner. A very slim chance, but one she was willing to take to save Hook.

"Hold the fuck up, Marce. No fuckin' way can I let you crawl out there in plain sight," Striker whispered.

"Then go distract Tanner, because there is no way you're keeping me from Hook." She gave Striker the most serious look she could muster with the high level of terror coursing through her. "We're wasting time."

If something happened to Hook before she had the chance to apologize, before she had an opportunity to tell him how much she loved him, the rest of her life would be completely worthless.

"Fuck," he muttered. "Okay, I'm going out there and I'll draw his attention away from this area. Move your ass as fast as you fuckin' can, babe." Striker dashed forward. "Hey, Tanner. Let's talk about this, man. No one has to get hurt here today." As he walked into the yard, he circled Tanner. "Why don't you let the girl go? She has nothing to do with this." Tanner's attention followed Striker as he moved toward the back of the yard.

"I'm unarmed, can't hurt you. Just let her go." He'd stowed his gun in the small of his back and held his hands up in a gesture of submission.

"No. Where's Marcie? I want her here, now." He waved the rifle around as he spoke and his innocent hostage whimpered.

The second Tanner's focus shifted from the house, Marcie scrambled forward on hands and knees, ignoring the sharp bite of rocks that ground into her palms and bare legs. She was too afraid to stand, too afraid of making noise and drawing Tanner's attention. When she reached the sliding glass door, she pried it open as slow as she dared. Time was not on her side.

"Okay, man. I think Marcie would be willing to talk with you if you dropped the gun." Striker increased his volume as she slid the door as if to block out the sound of the glass door gliding on the track. She slipped in the house and rose, her legs aching and quivering all at the same time. Without wasting a second, she raced toward Hook's office.

Wrapped around the doorknob, tied in what appeared ten knots, was a rope. The opposite end was tied with another obscene number of knots around the banister of the staircase across from the office. Hook had to be trapped inside. The rope was so tight around the doorknob, there wasn't a chance of unknotting it or slipping it off.

Maybe she could snap it with tension. "Hook!" she screamed as she crashed her shoulder against the door again and again. The only sound that greeted her cry was the crackle of flames. Dark gray smoke poured from the crack below the door, stinging her eyes and filling the air around her. Drawing in a full breath became difficult.

"Goddamn it!" she yelled, pushing against the door all her might. It didn't budge. "Please." Her voice was desperate to her own hears. Tears coursed down her cheeks and her lungs seized as deep coughs jolted her.

She dashed to the kitchen and grabbed the first sharp object she encountered, which happened to be a large butcher knife from the knife block. In no time, she was back at the office door, sawing through the rope like a madwoman. If there was a morsel of positivity in this fucked up situation, it was that the rope was thin and frayed with relative ease. With two hands wrapped around the knife handle, she drew it back and forth through the rope, over and over again. A primal roar erupted from her and with one last jerk, the rope split. Marcie landed hard on her bottom, but paid no attention to the pain in her tailbone. She dropped the knife and jumped to her feet and shoved the door open.

A blast of molten air and thick smoke slammed her as she stepped into the room. Her lungs immediately rejected the unclean air, throwing her into a painful coughing fit. She dropped to her knees in attempt to avoid the worst of the heat and smoke. With her hands in front of her and the flames licking her skin, she felt along the ground. Hook had to be in here. Why else would the door have been roped shut?

Her hand smacked into a cardboard box and for just a second, she froze. Jesus Christ. There was so much alcohol in here, the second the flames reached those boxes they were both deader than dead.

The room spun as her need for oxygen grew stronger, but she battled it. Miles of pure air waited just outside and she'd have it when she rescued Hook. Blindly reaching out, her hand encountered a man's heavy boot.

With a small sliver of hope, she rose to her feet. She couldn't see a damn thing and coughs racked her body continuously, but somehow she found the strength to grip Hook's feet and drag him toward the door.

Step after step she pulled him from the room and down the hall toward the front door of the house. Smoke now filled the hallway, but she'd spent enough time here to make her way without vision.

Just as she was mere feet from the front door, she slipped and fell to the ground. "Get up. You're so fucking close." Her voice was a raspy mess. She tried, she really and truly tried, but all strength had fled. Her legs refused to hold her and her hands slipped from Hooks boots each time she tried to tug him closer to the door.

"No." Sobs alternated with uncontrollable coughs until she could do nothing but curl on her side and ride out the wave of agony.

The sound of the front door slamming into the wall was the most welcome sound in the world. "Marcie?" Striker's voice was music to her ears.

"Here," she tried to call out, her raspy voice no match for the roar of the fire and the approaching sirens.

"Jesus Christ. Jester, get the fuck in here." Striker rushed in and crouched beside Marcie.

"Take Hook first." She doubled over as diaphragm spasms assaulted her again.

"Shhh, honey. We'll get him." He stroked her ash laden hair. "Jester, get Hook. I'll take Marcie."

"On it." Jester's booming voice cut through the roar of blood in her ears.

Seconds later, Marcie's eyes slammed shut as the daylight brightness became too much. Her instincts took over and tried to suck in fresh oxygen, but her lungs were too full of garbage and the most painful coughing spell attacked her.

"Shh, try to settle, hon. An ambulance just pulled in. We'll get you some help."

"Ta—" She let out a harsh cough. "Tanner?"

"You don't have to worry about him anymore, hon. I'll fill you in on it all later. Just concentrate on taking some deep breaths."

A few seconds later, the cool sheets from the gurney soothed her hot skin as Striker laid her down. She turned her head to see Hook laying on an identical gurney, his eyes closed, clothing singed and raw burns over parts of his arms. The oxygen mask on his face gave her hope that he was still alive, but her heart couldn't give up the fear of losing him just yet.

The EMTs worked on her, placing oxygen on her as well and assessing her vitals, but she tuned them out. All her remaining energy was focused on Hook, on willing the universe to allow him to wake up.

After what felt like an eternity, he jolted, his entire body rising from the gurney as horrible hacking coughs gripped him. As painful as it must have been for him, Marcie had never heard a sweeter sound in her life.

It meant Hook was alive.

It meant she had a chance to tell him she loved him.

CHAPTER FIFTEEN

Pain registered first. The biting sear of intense heat scorching his flesh. The stabbing pain in his abused lungs, starved for oxygen. Completely out of his control, Hook's muscles jerked and contracted over and over as his system tried to dispel the poison and replace it with oxygen.

Once he calmed enough that his brain could engage in thought, he immediately needed to know if Marcie was safe. He clawed at the mask over his nose and mouth. "Marcie?" His ravaged vocal cords wouldn't allow more than a weak croak. Men in uniform worked around him, ignoring his words.

Fuck that. Ensuring her safety was all that mattered. He struggled against strong hands that held him to the gurney.

"Hey, brother. Calm the fuck down. These guys are working to keep your ass on this earth another day. Cut them some slack." Jester's hulking form filled Hook's field of vision.

"Marcie?"

"She's all right, brother. Look to your left."

With great effort, Hook turned his head. Marcie lay on a gurney about ten feet away, a mask on her face as well. Their gazes locked and tears streamed from her beautiful green eyes. Damn she was gorgeous. Soot covered nearly every inch of her, except for two tracks of creamy skin trailing from her eyes.

"That's some girl you got there. She saved your dumb ass all by herself," Jester said.

He had no idea what the hell had happened, but there would be time to fill in the details later. Now, he'd let the paramedics work on him. Hell, he'd let them do whatever the fuck they needed to do to him. Marcie was alive and safe. He'd be able to hold her soon. That was all that mattered.

"Sir, you have a few extensive burns on your legs. We're going to give you some pain medicine now so it will have kicked in by the time we get you to the hospital. It will probably knock you out," the paramedic said.

That was fine. Marcie was safe. Nothing else was important. It wasn't long before the pain eased and darkness took him under yet again.

The next thing Hook knew, he was lying on crisp white sheets, in a sterile white room. Fogginess rimmed the edges of his consciousness, but he was alert enough to seek out Marcie. Sure enough, she sat sprawled in a high back, vinyl chair next to his hospital bed. Someone had given her a pair of green hospital scrubs and at some point, she'd showered, because the thick grime no longer covered her beautiful face.

Dark circles rimmed her eyes causing Hook's stomach to clench. They were due in part to the exhaustion and stress of the last few hours, but they'd been evident during the party as well. Owing to the fact that she'd been up all night stressing about their relationship instead of sleeping.

He took a deep breath through his nose, inhaling the oxygen provided by the hospital and couldn't hold back a wince. Damn, his chest felt like he'd gone three rounds with someone Jester's size and lost, badly. "Marcie?" Yikes, the hoarse rasp of his voice sounded like something out of a horror movie.

She lurched and her eyes flew open. "Hook!" With a wince of her own, she leaned over the bed. "Are you in pain? Do you need me to call the nurse? Are you thirsty? What can I do for you?"

"Whoa, baby, calm down." Her rapid-fire babbling had to be born of nerves and stress. "I'm okay. Now that I'm looking at you, I'm fine."

Tears filled her eyes and she clung to his hand. "Hook, God, it was so horrible. I was sure—" She shook her head. "I love you, Hook. I'm sorry. I'm screwing this up so bad. I just couldn't wait another to second to tell you. Today was too close. To think I almost lost you without telling you." A choked sob exploded from her and she shook as tears spilled down her face.

Her tears and anguish slayed him. In this moment, he wanted nothing more than to hold his woman in his arms and ease her mind. "Climb into bed with me."

With a hiccup, she shook her head. "I can't. You have some burns on your arms and legs that the doctor bandaged. I don't want to hurt you."

"You in this bed with me is the only thing that will make me feel better. I promise." He scooted over, masking a grimace of pain. No way could she stay in that damn chair. His woman's body against his was exactly the medicine he needed.

Moving gingerly, she climbed into the bed and settled against him, one arm across his stomach and her head on his shoulder.

With the head of the bed elevated, he was able to look down at her sad emerald eyes. "You were right, you know, Marcie."

A frown appeared. "Not that I don't love to hear that, but what was I right about?"

"You're so fucking strong and independent. And you can handle some serious shit without anyone's help. Jesus, Marcie, Jester told me you were the one to get me out of there. You saved my fucking life, babe. And by the way, I'm going to need those details."

A small sniff rose from her and she shook her head against his chest. "We'd both be dead if Striker and Jester hadn't found us at the end. And I realized something myself. I'm tired of doing everything alone. I use my independence to shield myself, but I want a partner. Someone to take care of me and someone for me to take care of."

Her words released a tension in him he hadn't realized had been building since their fight. "Any idea who you want to fill that position?"

She chuckled. "You're the only one I've ever wanted to take that job."

"Thank fuck." He pressed a kiss to her lips. It ended far before he was ready, but neither of their breathing was completely back to normal and they needed air before long. "I love you, Marcie. And I promise I won't walk in front of you, but stand beside you for the rest of your life."

"Hook…" Her voice was thick with emotion and love darkened her irises to a forest green.

"Christ, babe, don't look at me like that. We need to find a way to get me out of here as fast as possible because I need inside you. And soon."

"Sorry, buddy," she said. "Doc wants to keep you overnight."

"Fuck. Well then, I guess that gives you plenty of time to fill in the blanks and tell me what the fuck happened tonight."

CHAPTER SIXTEEN

"Tanner went crazy. That's what happened." Some of the all-consuming fear finally left her. Hook was alive, awake, and aside from a few scars that would linger on his legs, expected to make a full recovery.

And he loved her.

"He started spraying bullets around the backyard and took some poor club girl hostage. Striker kept me safe, but when I smelled smoke, I knew you were in danger." Tears threatened to fall again, but she managed to hold them at bay this time. "Um, Striker distracted him while I snuck into the house. After that, I missed everything that went down in the backyard, but from what I understand, Striker goaded him until he was so riled he lost his focus. That gave your friends Jester and Gumby enough time to take him down. From what they told me, the cops showed up then and took custody of Tanner."

Hook tightened his grip around her and dropped a kiss on the top of her heard. "What happened inside?"

"The door to your office was tied shut with a rope from the doorknob to the stair rail. It took me forever to get it to budge. God, Hook, I was terrified. I could feel the heat, see and smell the smoke. I knew you were in there but I couldn't get to you. It was so awful."

There went the ability to hold back the tears. They poured from her eyes, soaking Hook's hospital gown. "Shh, baby, it's over. I'm fine. Because of you. Because of how fucking fierce and brave you are."

His words registered, but now that she'd opened the floodgates, the story tumbled out between sobs. "Finally, I moved the chair and opened the door. It was hot. So hot. I couldn't see, couldn't breathe. The only thing I could do was crawl around on the floor, so that's what I did. Eventually I bumped into you and I dragged you out of the room. The goal was to get you out the front door, but I didn't make it. Striker and Jester rescued us."

Hook's hold on her tightened to the point of uncomfortable, but she didn't say anything. Nothing was more important than being close to him in this moment. "Babe, I know I said you were strong, and fierce, and so fucking brave, but if you ever put yourself in danger like that again I won't be held responsible for my actions."

One eyebrow rise and she glanced up at him. "Oh really? What are you going to do about it?"

"You think I'm joking? You could have been killed, Marcie. I promise you, if you ever do something that foolish again, I'll tie you to my bed and fuck you so hard you won't be able to leave for a week."

"Hmmm, maybe you shouldn't wait until the next time I put myself in danger to dole out that punishment."

"You think this is funny, woman?"

He sounded truly upset so she stopped teasing him. "No, Hook. I don't, but your life was in danger. I love you. I had no choice but to try to save you. Your house was burning all around you—oh my God! Your house! You worked so hard on it. There was so much damage."

He'd purchased that house when it was in ruins and spent years rehabbing it. Her heart hurt to think of all his labor wiped out in one evening by her crazy ex.

"You think I give a fuck about the house? Seriously?"

"But your blood, sweat, and tears are in that house."

"Yeah and your blood was almost in that house. Burn the fucking thing to the ground for all I care. I'm not sure I could live there again knowing you came so close to dying."

"I'm sorry I brought this horror into your life." Guilt was heavy in her stomach.

"Woman, are you trying to piss me off?"

His outraged tone only served to make her laugh. "You really do love me, don't you?"

"Yes, I fucking love you," he said in the same livid voice. "What the hell do I have to do to prove that to you?"

She rose on her elbow and kissed him for all she was worth. "Get better very fast so you can dish out my punishment."

He growled against her lips. "Yes, ma'am."

"I love you too, TJ."

"Damn straight, you do," he said before he captured her lips in another sizzling kiss.

She'd thought giving her heart to Hook meant giving up her independence and autonomy. She couldn't have been more wrong. It meant gaining a partner, a lover, a champion.

And that was everything.

Thank you so much for spending some time in the No Prisoners' world. If you enjoyed the book please feel free to leave a review on Amazon or Goodreads.

Keep reading for a preview of **STRIKER**, Book 1 of the No Prisoners MC Series

Join Lilly's mailing list for a free 9000 word novella: A No Prisoners Wedding.
www.lillyatlas.com

No Prisoners MC Series
Hook: A No Prisoners MC Novella
Striker
Jester
Acer
Lucky
Snake

Trident Ink
Escapades

Hell's Handlers MC
Zach
Maverick

Hook

Jigsaw
Copper

The doors to Desert Community Hospital slid open with a whoosh. It was a sound Dr. Lila Emerson heard countless times each shift, so she didn't bother to look up, focusing instead on completing a written proposal for the concussion and sports safety program she hoped to institute at the local high school. Another forty-five minutes and she would have it completed, and be on her way home to the bottle of Cabernet and warm bath that promised to soothe her tired body after a hectic week. She couldn't wait.

"Stitch." Jester's booming voice bellowed through the lobby. "We need you, girl! Gumby's face is all busted up."

Lila groaned. Again? Perhaps the man needed a new nickname. Gumby didn't seem fitting, considering the number of times his body cracked.

Members of the No Prisoners motorcycle club had burst into the lobby of the emergency room. She could always tell the moment they came through the doors, even without the inevitable *we're here* announcement made by Jester. There was a change in the energy of the room: a charge of fear and distrust from some, a nervous respect from others, and a buzz of sexual energy from all the testosterone they seemed to emit. There was a strong possibility she was the only one who noticed that last point.

Jester led the pack of two leather-clad, boot-wearing men as they tromped through the waiting room, and up to the admissions desk. Silence descended as the patients awaiting treatment gaped at the intimidating duo. Jester was a mountain of a man, topping out at no less than six foot five inches, and probably weighed close to three hundred pounds of solid muscle. He had the body type of a serious weight lifter, and could have been one, for all she knew about him. Both arms boasted full sleeves of tattoos, and additional ink peeked out from the collar of his T-shirt. Jester's dark brown hair was long, past his shoulders, and thick, though usually contained in a ponytail at the base of his neck. He was a formidable figure, and not someone she'd want to meet in a back alley at night, despite his apparent jovial demeanor.

He reached the admissions desk, and braced his meaty hands on the counter. The action placed him directly above poor Anna, the middle aged receptionist who worked the night shift. She had to tilt her head way back to meet Jester's fierce gaze.

"Um, if you wouldn't mind filling out these papers." Anna's voice shook as she fumbled with the clipboard that contained the intake paperwork. "Then please have a seat, and we will call you back soon. There are only a few patients ahead of you, so the wait shouldn't be more than an hour."

"That's not gonna work for us. We'll just head back to an empty room, and Stitch can meet us in there."

Jester was the first to call her Stitch, after a number of club members had required stitches following a particularly brutal bar brawl one night a few months ago. The moniker stuck, and spread throughout the town.

The No Prisoners. Their name came from the phrase *take no prisoners*, an expression the club was rumored to live by. Lila's patients loved to pass along town gossip, and she was regaled with numerous grandiose stories about the club's penchant for making their enemies disappear. Typically, she took what patients told and believed about half of it, but these rumors she didn't doubt. Each club member she'd met was able to laugh and joke with her, but there was always a deadly undercurrent that couldn't be ignored. They all carried weapons, and she'd often wondered how they got them past the security guard, but she wasn't about to ask. No point in getting on their bad side.

Lila rolled her eyes, and stood, intending to intervene on Anna's behalf, when her gaze landed on the man rounding out the group. Striker shook hands with the night security guard as he came through the double doors. In its typical fashion, her heart rate kicked up a notch at the sight of the No Prisoners' vice president.

Her eyes widened as she watched Striker pass what looked like money to the portly guard who glanced around before sliding his hand into his back pocket. Well that explained how they got their arsenal in the building, and why they were never asked to leave, no matter how many patients complained of being uncomfortable by their presence.

If Webster's had a definition for sexy bad boy there would be a picture of Striker. He stood around six-foot-two, with muscles galore and dark, almost black hair that was short and a bit unruly. Combined with a strong jaw, piercing blue eyes, and leather, he made for one mouthwatering package.

"Ah, there's no guarantee that, um, Dr. Emerson will be the one to see you." Anna's face was flushed, her voice wavered, and her eyes shone with a glimmer of unshed tears. Jester still hovered over her, a scowl on his face.

Lila sighed. Her schedule had been crazy this week and she'd had to squeeze in work on the proposal anywhere she could. It was just about finished, and she had planned on it being done by the time this shift was over. So much for that.

She moved toward the reception area to rescue Anna before the unassuming woman broke down under Jester's glower. "Anna, it's okay." Lila put a hand on the older woman's shoulder. "There's no one else in line to check in. Why don't you run and grab a cup of coffee from the break room, and I'll get these gentlemen's information and get them settled."

The look of relief on Anna's face was almost comical, and she scurried away the second the offer was out of Lila's mouth. The club members were imposing for sure, but in all the times they'd been into the ER, Lila could be honest in saying they never actually caused any trouble. They just always looked like they were on the verge of it. Still, the patients in the waiting room stared at the floor and out the windows, anywhere but at the hulking men in leather and chains. Most of the staff reacted the same way, and Lila realized, aside from the worthless security guard, she was alone in the shared admissions and charting area.

She shifted her attention to the three men standing by the desk. Jester wore an ear-to-ear grin on his face, like flustering the receptionist had been the highlight of his evening. Gumby, the injured party, stood next to him and held a blood soaked rag under a rapidly swelling eye. Striker leaned against the wall off to the side, arms crossed, face unreadable, and Lila forced her attention away from him.

"Just head on back to room four," she instructed. It was best to get them taken care of quickly. Tension would leave the ER once they were back outside on their motorcycles. Plus, she'd be able to go home as soon as she treated Gumby. "You know the way. I have to talk to the nurse for a minute and we'll be right in. Try not to scare away too much of our business on your way back there."

"Aww, Stitch, Gumby's face doesn't look that bad," Jester said.

"I was talking to you," she shot back with a smile.

Jester laughed, threw an arm around Gumby's shoulders, and steered him in the direction Lila had indicated. Striker lingered at the admissions desk. When she met his gaze, one corner of his mouth lifted in the arrogant grin she had come to expect from him. Her breath caught in her throat and she forgot what she was supposed to be doing. She barely remembered her own name when he looked at her like that, and lately the heated gazes seemed to be coming more frequently.

Part of Lila, the part that had moved across the country in hope of having the freedom to live her life her way, told her she loved the attention. She was free to make her own decisions for the first time in her life. Taking this job in a small town hospital where she could really affect the lives of individuals in her community was the first step in exerting her autonomy. The next step would be finding a man to spend that life with.

She really didn't know Striker, but the idea of the tough-looking biker wanting a picket fence and two point five kids was almost laughable. Lila could admire the attractive packaging from afar, but she shouldn't be thinking about the desire that shone in his eyes, as she did far too often. There was nothing but trouble down that road. Especially since he probably spent much of his time on the wrong side of the law.

"So, Doc, I hear you have a big presentation coming up," he said.

Pride swelled with the knowledge that there was talk around town about her program. It was her baby. She'd seen too many high school athletes come through the ER with serious head injuries due to the school's ignorance about concussions and equipment safety.

"I do! I'm presenting my idea in front of the school board Monday night. If all goes well, I'll form a committee and begin putting a program together. It's so important. Did you know that the majority of the sports equipment at the high school is over ten years old? There is no way it is in any condition to keep the kids protected."

Her face heated. She was passionate about this project, and could talk about it for hours, to anyone apparently, even sexy bikers who normally had her tongue-tied. "Sorry. I can ramble on about this until your ears fall off. I'm sure you're not interested, so I should probably go tend to the bleeding man."

She turned to flee toward the treatment rooms, but stopped when Striker's voice sounded behind her. "Actually, Doc, some of my guys have kids in the high school. A few of them play football. I think it's great what you're doing."

And damn if her heart didn't do a happy dance at the look of admiration on his face. With a nod in his direction, she turned and headed down the hall.

Cammie, her friend and one of the best ER nurses she'd ever worked with, came up the hall as Lila went down it. "Cammie, can you grab a suture kit and meet me in room four? I'll also need lidocaine and saline to irrigate the wound. Looks like Gumby took quite a shot to the face."

At the mention of Gumby's name, Cammie paled a bit, but she nodded and walked straight toward the supply room. Lila wasn't sure what that was about, and didn't want to waste time speculating.

She pushed the door to exam room four open and walked in. The minuscule room was even smaller than usual with two very large males filling the space. Gumby sat on the treatment table directly opposite the door, the blood soaked cloth still pressed to his face. Jester was off to the side, sitting in a plastic chair that was built for a man half his size. Striker hadn't followed her into the room, and she breathed a small sigh of relief at the lack of distraction.

"Hi, Doc. Miss me?" Gumby asked. He tried to smile but winced when the action caused the skin around his still expanding eye to crinkle.

"Hey there, Gumby, I see you're here for our standing Friday night date. I gotta tell you, it wouldn't hurt to bring a girl flowers every once in a while," she said with a wink.

Jester laughed. "You may want to take it easy on Gumb tonight, Stitch. Not only is his pretty face all busted, he got his ass handed to him in the ring. He's been a tad cranky ever since."

"Fuck off, Jest," grumbled Gumby. "Fucker got in a few lucky shots."

"Sure he did, Gumb." Jester patted him on the back like he might a petulant child, and shot a quick wink Lila's way.

"Lie down on your back for me please, you are way too tall for me to reach your face all the way up there." She adjusted the angle on the treatment table as she spoke, so he wouldn't be flat, but would lay at about a thirty-degree incline.

Gumby did as she asked while Lila donned a pair of nitrile gloves. Before she moved to assess him, she opened a drawer beneath the table, and pulled out a few four-by-fours of gauze and ripped the packages open. When Gumby was in position, Lila placed her gloved hand over his to remove the saturated cloth.

His eye was badly contused and swollen shut. The color palette was spectacular. Various shades of purple and blue mottled the skin surrounding his entire orbit. A two-inch laceration stretched across Gumby's cheekbone as well. The gash cut deep, but not jagged, so it would be easy to approximate the edges and he'd have minimal scarring. She pressed the clean gauze over his eye while she waited for Cammie to bring the suture kit.

"Did you get knocked out, Gumby? If so I'll need to do a CT scan of your head."

"I'm good, Stitch. Just need my face sewn up so it will stop fucking bleeding."

"Well, I'd really like to—"

"Doc." A gruff voice came from over her shoulder. "He's fine, just do your thing, and put his face back together so we can get out of your way."

She'd heard him approach and had tried to ignore the star of too many of her late night fantasies, but apparently Striker wasn't going to let that happen. A dueling sizzle of awareness and annoyance struck her as he stepped in between her and her patient.

"Thank you, Striker. As usual I'd be lost in my job without your sound medical input."

"Man, I love coming here." Jester laughed. "Too bad one of us needs to get all jacked up or I'd be here every day to be on the receiving end of your charms, Stitch."

Lila turned her attention back to Striker, and narrowed her eyes to let him know she was serious when she expressed her dislike of his interference. Once again she was met with a one-sided smirk she would like to smack off his face. Okay, there was a chance she'd like to kiss the smirk off his face, but she wasn't ready to admit that out loud.

Hook

Cammie knocked on the door before she entered, and wheeled in a cart with the supplies Lila had requested. Lila often teased her about her curly red hair and how it bounced as she walked, mimicking her bubbly personality, but tonight she was stiff and rigid as though she was being walked to her doom. "I have your suture kit, Dr. Emerson. What can I do to help you?" she asked.

"Thanks, Cammie, I can take it from here."

Cammie shot Lila a grateful smile, and was out of the room in a flash, apparently not wanting to miss out on the reprieve she was given. Lila made a mental note to ask Cammie why she seemed so uncomfortable when Jester mumbled. "Yeah, Gumby, probably shouldn't have climbed on that ride, knowing how often you end up here."

Well, that explained why Cammie lit out of there like the floor was caving in. Given how the members of the MC flirted with any female staff between ages nineteen and fifty, she was surprised there weren't more awkward encounters.

Lila gifted Gumby with an innocent grin. "Oh crap! I'm so sorry, Gumby, I forgot I have a meeting to get to. I'm just going to call Cammie back and have her stitch you up. I'm sure she won't forget to numb you, and she'll be very gentle." Her snarky statement would have been better believed if she hadn't burst out laughing halfway through at the look of horror on Gumby's face.

Behind her, Striker laughed. "Ouch, Doc, way to hit the man when he's down."

Lila chuckled. She always had fun when these guys were here. "Okay let's get down to business so you can get out of here, and ignore my instructions by mixing your pain killers with booze." She grabbed the bottle of sterile saline off the cart, and irrigated the wound. Gumby hissed out a curse. "Sorry, Gumby. I can't see exactly how deep it is unless I clean out the blood. There's a chance you have an orbital fracture. I recommend a CT."

He shook his head. "Just close it up."

Surprise, surprise. "Sometimes you guys are very annoying."

They all laughed, and she used the lidocaine to deaden the area around the wound. When he was numb, she ripped open the suture kit and got to work. Lila could feel Striker's eyes on her back and she had to concentrate to keep her hands from quivering like a third year medical student. Thankfully they remained quiet, allowing her to focus, and in ten minutes Gumby's wound was closed, the stitch job quite impressive, if she did say so herself.

"Okay, Gumby, you are the proud new recipient of fifteen stitches. I'll have a nurse bring you something for the pain. It will hurt like a bitch when the lidocaine wears off. The nurse will also have your discharge instructions. You can leave when she's done."

Lila knew how they operated, and didn't expect a single instruction to be followed, but protocol was protocol and she'd obey it. As she turned to leave the room, her gaze collided with Striker's. His heated stare affected her more than she was prepared to admit so she shifted her gaze and broke the connection. Neither said anything as she left the room, but she felt the lingering effects of having him so near in her racing heart and wobbly legs.

Her shift was officially over, and she could go home as soon as Gumby's paperwork was complete. Now she just needed to get Striker off her mind long enough to finish her proposal and still get some sleep tonight.

About the Author

Lilly Atlas is a contemporary romance author. She's a proud Navy wife and mother of three spunky girls. Every time Lilly downloads a new eBook she expects her Kindle App to tell her it's exhausted and overworked, and to beg for some rest. Thankfully that hasn't happened yet so she can often be found absorbed in a good book.

Made in the USA
Middletown, DE
27 June 2023